The Apology

Christian TeBordo

Astrophil Press

at University of South Dakota

2021

Layout and design by duncan b. barlow

Edited by McCormick Templeman and Christian TeBordo

Additional Proofreading: Juliet Clark

Astrophil Press at University of South Dakota
1st pressing 2021

Library of Congress Cataloging-in-Publication Data
Christian TeBordo
p. cm.
ISBN 978-0-9980199-5-6 (pbk. : paper)
1.Fiction, American
Library of Congress Control Number: 9780998019956

http://www.astrophilpress.com

"Truth cannot be imparted," said Kline. "It must be inflicted."

Brian Evenson, **Dark Property**

"But as my poor left-handed friend used to put it: philosophic speculation is the invention of the rich. Down with it."

~~Hermann~~ Vladimir Nabokov, **Despair**

"Yet it would really be worth knowing if one could poeticize oneself out of a girl in such a way as to make her so proud that she imagined it was she who was bored with the relationship."

~~Johannes the Seducer A Victor Eremita~~ Soren Kierkegaard, **Either/Or**

The Philosophical Apology of Mike Long, a.k.a Michael Rider, a.k.a. Knight Rider

or

Chemical Warfare in the Workplace

or

Male Pattern Blindness

or

Look at That Guy with the Head.

or

The Concept of Irony with a Single Reference to John Ashcroft

or

I Am Terror's Son (Maybe)

I

I'll explain the chemical weapons later, but if you want to get to the bottom of this stalking business you should talk to Kit Carson, the computer guy. That's his real name—Kit Carson. I called him KC because Kit Carson is too stupid a name to repeat, and he almost never complained about it.

KC was the one who organized the Friday night happy hour and tried to make it sound to the new girl in payable like we always got together Friday nights after work, especially weeks when someone new started, to get to know her, he meant, them, even though he'd never shown any company pride before and had probably been directly responsible for the failure of my previous attempts at community building, like the office scavenger hunt and the adopt-a-highway program. Two years later they were still finding staplers in weird places and our stretch of I-76 looked pathetic. It was embarrassing.

I was suspicious even before the whole happy hour charade. In fact, I was on to him from day one. It was only about halfway to lunch on Monday morning and KC was already on his way back from his second cigarette break. I saw him coming from down the hall and tried to look busy because he was doing that walk that means he thinks he's the Sultan of Software—I've actually heard him use the phrase out loud—and I didn't want to hear about how he made short work of some installation that was giving everybody else all kinds of trouble, which is boring and I don't understand a word of it anyway. Except this time he didn't want to talk about information technology. This time he wanted to talk about something I understand perfectly well, which is women.

I was finishing up an email, an important response to an important message, and told myself not to look at him.

Just stare at the monitor.

I looked at him.

"Porn again?" he said, and cracked up.

That one never stopped being funny for him. I rolled my eyes and minimized my browser.

"Business," I said.

He rolled *his* eyes.

"I told you it's a scam," he said.

If you listened to KC everything was a scam. It made you wonder how he thought anyone ever caught a break. I mean, it's not like you just sit at some desk until one day you suddenly turn into Horatio Alger.

"You don't even know what it says," I said.

"Lemme guess," he said. "Your long-lost uncle won the lottery in the UK but he died before he could pick up the money."

Ask somebody's advice about a proposition from some Nigerians one time and you'll never hear the end of it.

"Never mind," I said.

"Think of it this way," said KC, "if anybody's offering to do *anything* with you at all it's a scam, because no one would trust you with anything business-wise. You're an idiot."

In a sense he had a reason to think I was an idiot when it came to business. For a while after I asked him about the email from the Nigerians—this was probably my first month in the office—he would stop and ask me who was trying to hand me their millions every time he saw me looking at my computer.

"Where's the big money coming from today?" he'd ask. "Shenzhen? Budapest? Pyongyang?"

One Monday morning I got fed up and said, "This guy I know from college."

"He as dumb as you?" said KC.

"He's a chemist," I said. "He has an idea that's gonna make us both rich."

Mention a scientist and everything changes.

"What's the idea?" he said.

There was no idea, just like there was no scientist.

"I'm supposed to just give it away?" I said.

"I don't know anything about chemicals," he said.

"But that's the thing," I said. "It's so simple, we can't believe no one's ever thought of it before."

KC pulled up a chair, sat down.

"Maybe I can help," he said. "Build a website or something."

"Actually, we might be able to use you," I said. "My friend does all the technical stuff; I'm doing marketing, the face of the operation. We could use an IT guy."

"So what is it?" he said.

I looked around to make sure we were alone and leaned forward.

"You ever notice how pretty much every household cleaner uses either ammonia or chlorine bleach?" I said.

He nodded.

"Don't you think it would be even better if you combined them into the most powerful cleaning product known to man?" I said.

He broke out with a big, slow smile, mouth so wide the fur of his Vandyke almost reached his ears.

"We call it ChlorAmmo," I said.

He walked away like he had a newfound respect for me and was nice and considerate the rest of the day, but the next morning he stormed up to my desk and yell-whispered: "Poison!"

He was right. When you combine chlorine and ammonia you get chlorine gas. Chlorine gas will slip into your lungs, especially in poorly ventilated spaces, and react with whatever water's in there to form hydrochloric acid, which everybody knows corrodes human tissue, meaning it can burn or eat you from inside out.

Unless you have more ammonia in the mixture than bleach. That makes hydrazine, which they use in rocket fuel. It mostly gets at you through direct contact with your mucus membranes, but even inhaling its fumes can be dangerous over long periods of time. That hardly matters because it's highly unstable and will probably explode in your face before you get a chance to sniff at it.

But I couldn't admit I knew that.

"What are you talking about?" I said.

"ChlorAmmo?" he said. "It's poison."

"Everything's poisonous when you use it wrong," I said. "You don't swallow bleach or take a bath in ammonia or vice versa. Everything has its proper use, including ChlorAmmo, under the right circumstances. It could clean up a lot of messes."

Science again. KC backed off, but he wasn't nice to me this time; he just avoided me the rest of the day.

And then he didn't come in the next day. Or the next day. Or the next. He might have called in sick, but nobody told me, and I started to worry that he'd tried to mix chlorine and ammonia himself, at home, with a bucket and some rubber gloves or something.

I alternated between feeling guilty for giving him the idea and feeling like it served him right for trying to steal it, until he came in the next Monday morning like nothing unusual had happened. I didn't ask him where he'd been and he didn't say, but after that he shied away from the scams, stuck to asking me about porn, unless I was idiot enough to mention business.

"Anyway, that's not why I'm here," he said.

"No," I said, "you're here to work. Or you should be."

"Actually I work over there," he said pointing to a cubicle across the room. "I'm here," he pointed at my desk, "to ask you," he pointed at me, "if you've seen the new girl," he pointed his thumb over his shoulder and down the hall, "in payable."

"You mean woman?" I said. "Or are we suddenly breaking child labor laws and you're some kind of pervert?"

He rolled his eyes again and walked over to his cubicle without looking back.

I was just being obnoxious. I knew what he meant. What I didn't know was why he'd asked me if I'd seen the new girl in payable. Was it just a casual who's the new girl? Was she particularly attractive or particularly ugly? With some fantastic deformity? My curiosity was piqued, but I couldn't give KC the satisfaction of showing it by walking down the hall, checking her out, and reporting back immediately.

It was a long wait for lunch. I couldn't keep my mind on the email I was writing. One minute I was wracking my brain for the perfect closing salutation and the next I was imagining some shady and complicated business involving poor but noble Eastern European peasants who dressed sort of medieval, and international slave traders with bleached blond hair and an eye patch here and there; a long trip in a dark, dank shipping container with several catastrophes along the way, over which a certain pure, young, once-peasant, now apparently white slave girl's indomitable spirit prevails because of her beauty and her innocence; and finally the arrival in a certain American city known for brotherly love and also its former excellence in slave trading, where only the most beautiful and pure of them—that same peasant girl who had overcome so much in the crossing—would be sold to payable, where her job would be to satisfy the sordid desires of important businessmen and clients. But she would resist the advances of these sleazy fat cats, finding herself irresistibly attracted to a lowly office manager who felt the need to go to lunch a little early.

I mention this little indiscretion with the early lunch so you know I'm being completely candide.

I STOPPED INTO PAYABLE ON MY WAY OUT, just to see if anybody needed anything.

"I've got some errands to run. Urgent stuff," I said, looking around and peering over cubicles, which isn't too hard for me because I'm on the tall side. "So I'm heading to lunch a little early. Anybody need anything?"

There were a couple of grunts, a head shake or two, maybe a *no thanks*, but I didn't press the issue because I didn't see anyone in there I didn't recognize and I didn't actually want to get anybody anything. I figured the new girl must be at lunch already, in which case, if she wanted to keep her new job, she'd be back by the time I got back from mine.

I left.

But you have to take the elevator to get to street level from our office unless you want to walk down seventeen floors in business shoes, which is enough to make your knees creak aloud just thinking about it, and the restrooms are a little to the left of the elevators, and I thought maybe I'd been wrong about the new girl already being at lunch; maybe she was just answering the call of nature, which is perfectly natural, even if you don't like to think about such a pure and innocent thing doing it.

There was a ding and the elevator door opened arrow pointing downward as I stood there imagining the new girl in payable on the toilet, and before I realized it the door was closing and the elevator was moving on. I decided I'd wait a minute to push the button again. I didn't want the elevator to get worn out, which is a thing I'm very sensitive to, because, as the only office manager, I myself am always being pulled in a million different directions, and also because one time I got stuck in there for about three hours on the way up one morning, and when they finally got me out I'd had it and decided it called for a mental health day, but my boss, Ms. Miles, docked me eight vacation hours instead, and what could I do about it? Get it down to five, that's all, since at least the first three weren't my fault.

The new girl was taking a long time in the bathroom and it was starting to creep me out to tell the truth. I wondered what she could be doing in there. Maybe I inched a little closer to the door, but it's not like I was about to put my ear to it or anything when a voice behind me said: "What are you doing there?"

I jolted into her—I could tell it was a her by the voice and by the feel of her enormous, matronly breasts against my shoulder blades—and almost knocked her over. I probably would have knocked her over if I hadn't spun around and grabbed her huge, flabby arm just in time. Rita. The receptionist.

"Rita!" I said.

She was looking straight at me, but she turned her head so she could look at me out of the corner of her eye. Not a word of thanks. As if I'd meant to knock her over.

"What are you doing?" she said in a tone that said whatever I'd been doing was wrong.

"Waiting for the elevator," I said. "You?"

"Going to the ladies'," she said, like ladies' was an exclusive club where I wasn't welcome.

I nodded, stood there to show I was comfortable with my version of what I'd been doing and make sure she was, too. She kept at it with the corner-vision, made an out-of-my-way gesture with one fat hand. I looked over my shoulder, noticed I was sort of half-blocking her way into the women's room, more if you account for her size, and edged toward the elevator bank so she'd see that's what I'd been there for all along. She made a big production of turning sideways and sucking in as if to show I still hadn't given her enough room or had forced her to eat three pieces of cake at the last office birthday party, and kept her eye on me until she was all the way in with the door closed behind her like she was worried I was going to follow her in and molest her or something. If you've ever laid eyes on Rita, you know that would never cross my mind, even if you haven't laid eyes on me. I'm cute enough, believe it or not. Just ask Bonnie Barstow.

I heard the lock click behind Rita and realized the new girl hadn't been in there after all, unless this was some lesbian tryst. But what kind of white slave peasant ingénue would be arranging elaborate lesbian trysts after only one morning at work? And with Rita? That's just stupid.

I checked my phone and saw my lunch break was already half up. No time to wait for the elevator, and besides, I didn't want to risk being there when Rita got out. I took the stairs and my knees started creaking, grinding really, before I'd made it two flights.

I'D PRETTY MUCH FORGOTTEN ABOUT the new girl in payable by the time I got back, but I had to pass Rita to get to my desk. I shuddered at the thought of their little bathroom rendezvous even though the rendezvous was just my imagination. Rita was on the phone, probably with some friend, which is against company policy. I nodded as I walked past and got the evil eye for my efforts.

I stopped into payable again, but still I didn't see anyone I didn't recognize, didn't see anyone at all at first. I stepped all the way into the room and stood on tiptoes to look over the cubicles. One of the reps was in his cubicle in the far corner, leaning back in his chair with his feet up on his desk, gnawing on something wrapped in plastic.

I said: "Edward," and he almost fell over backward.

Edward is jumpy like that. He's missing his left ring finger above the second knuckle because someone surprised him while he was using the paper cutter a couple years back. I didn't see it happen, but I was there for the aftermath and I was the one with the presence of mind to put the finger on ice. Unfortunately, the paper cutter's blade was dull and the finger ended up being too mangled to reattach. Don't ask me what anybody in payable was doing with the paper cutter in the first place because I don't know and don't want to.

After that I bought a whetstone on my own dime, and I've kept the paper cutter sharp ever since.

Edward pulled himself together and put his feet on the floor.

"You scared me," he said.

Everything scares Edward.

I walked over to his cubicle so I didn't have to keep standing there on my toes to see him. There was a little bag of potato chips on his desk. Rap Snacks brand. B-B-Q-in' wit my Honey.

"Where is everybody?" I said.

"Lunch," he said.

"How come you're here?" I said.

"Someone's gotta man the phones," he said.

"Isn't that the new girl's job?" I said.

"She's at lunch too," he said.

I nodded.

"She doesn't seem to be working out, does she," I said.

"You've met her?" he said.

I couldn't understand why everyone was so concerned with whether I'd seen the new girl or not. Like if I'd met her I'd understand why it would be okay to take an absurdly long lunch on her very first day.

"What's that got to do with anything?" I said.

Edward relaxed, or got as relaxed as he gets. He leaned back, put his feet on the desk again, making sure to avoid his bag of chips, and crossed his arms.

"You haven't met her," he said.

"Just tell her I need to see her when she gets back if she ever does," I said. "I have to show her where we keep the supplies and how to put in a request if we get too low on anything."

He tried to smile but it came off like a grin. You could tell he was having trouble keeping his chair back to look casual by the way his knees were trembling.

"Rita took care of it already," he said.

"Rita?" I said.

He finally gave up, swung his legs down, let his chair tip forward.

"Showed her around before you got in this morning," he said.

Rita comes in a half hour before anyone else, in case some early bird calls up. We don't want them thinking we don't have things covered. But thirty minutes is thirty minutes. Even if the new girl was there right when Rita showed, it was hardly enough time for a thorough tour of the office. There are supply closets in out of the way places, first aid kits only I know how to find. Edward should appreciate that.

"Rita wouldn't know a post-it note from a paper clip," I said.

Edward shrugged. It made me want to go grab the paper cutter, bring it back, and slice another finger off clean. Or bash him over the head with the gridded surface until his face was bloody graph paper. But I didn't. Instead I reached into the bag on his desk, grabbed a chip, and shoved it in my mouth menacingly.

"You want the whole bag?" he said. "I'm supposed to be on a diet."

I looked him up and down. He was the skinniest person in the office, ectomorphic from pop-veined forehead to clammy blue toes. I'm guessing about the toes.

"I don't wanna catch diabetes," he said. "It's a death sentence."

"I just wanted the one," I said.

I turned and headed for the door. Before the hallway I stopped, looked back, stood tippy-toe as casual as I could.

"Just send her my way," I said.

I could only see the nut of his head bobbing above the edge of his cubicle; couldn't tell if he was jittering or giggling.

"I told you," he said. "Rita already showed her."

"Fine," I said, like that was exactly what I'd wanted, one last thing I had to worry about.

I held my head low and kept my eyes on the ground on the way back to my desk because I didn't want to talk to anyone else, but KC was in the common area eating his lunch, and he caught me as I tried to get by.

"You see her yet?" he said.

"Yeah," I said, still moving, not looking up. "She's a dog."

"What!" said KC.

He believed me, but he didn't get up from his Rubbermaid tub of whatever-it-was to argue.

I didn't bother checking my email or phone when I got to my desk. I was totally consumed by the new girl situation. But not in a stalkerish way. In a what-the-fuck-is-going-on-around-here-and-why-is-everyone-else—everyone-else-including-Rita-who-just-did-not-seem-the-type-until-that-morning—behaving-stalkerish-about-this-new-girl way.

Time passes quicker when you're stewing like that, and soon KC was done with his lunch, was rinsing his feedbag out in the kitchenette sink, which it was not really equipped for. It's not like there was a garbage disposal to grind down the leftover chunks of Beefaroni KC didn't hoover up, and that's why it was always clogging. And who had to fix that? Me, that was who. It was enough to make me wish ChlorAmmo really existed, to clean the whole mess up.

When he was done he walked by my desk and I couldn't help but look his way. I guess he still believed I really had seen the new girl, because all he did was shake his head like a disappointed older brother in a movie, my only experience of older brothers because I don't have one, or younger, or a sister of any age for that matter.

My big bro walked past and on to his cubicle without saying anything. It made me sad, for me, and mostly for him, who, at least for the moment, was playing the role of guy whose only goal was to teach me to act right for once, and I couldn't do anything but let him down.

Then I remembered that KC was a total asshole, and also realized there was a bright side even if he wasn't, namely, that his disappointment could only have been the result of my having called her a dog. The fact that he reacted that way allowed for just one possibility—that she was anything but a dog. If she was a not particularly unattractive woman, with, for example, snaggleteeth or red hair, both of which I myself am partial to, though not in the same person, my comment would have led to what passed, with KC, for witty repartee. If she had very plump lips and very pale skin, which I'm also partial to, in any female person, one or another or both, and I had called her a dog, KC would have been his usual nasty self, which would have been his way of saying different strokes for different folks. If she'd just been ugly, he would have been similarly nasty by way of telling me her sheer hideousness called for a more creative comment.

He'd narrowed the possibilities without meaning to, and that was a point for me, which would lead to more points for me because now I could add by that subtraction. It's called deductive reasoning. Start with the new girl in payable could not possibly be a dog, and because every kindergartner knows what a dog is, the only question left is what a dog is not. She could not, for instance, be repulsive by any definition. That left a pretty wide spectrum. But. She also could not be unconventionally attractive as in the above examples. One man's trash etc. She had to be the kind of person who could please all the male gazes all the time, some more than others, of course.

She had to be white. White was a given. Any other color could have left things open to debate for a guy like KC. Which isn't to say she couldn't be tan. Or the shade of orange that passes for tan among certain white people these days.

She couldn't be too thin and she couldn't be fat. Either is a potential dealbreaker in some circles. Likewise tits and ass. She had to have some of each and not too much of either, though given KC's whiteness, the type of bar he likes to frequent, the secret file of downloads he keeps on the office server, I'd suspect more of the former than the latter.

She was probably blond. Contrary to cliché, not all gentlemen prefer them, but those who don't aren't offended by them. And eye color? Who cares? Anyone who says otherwise reads women's magazines in hopes it'll help him seduce the dumber ones.

When it all came down, there were really only two possibilities—virgin and whore. Of course, there was the rare possibility that she could be both, like in a Russian novel, but why would someone so gifted be in our office? At the same time, she couldn't be all that good of one or the other. She had to be office hot, the kind of girl that looks like an NFL cheerleader girl, after a three or four beer happy hour.

Not exactly my type, but I would have done her, even before seeing her, and I'm not giving up now. This retreat is tactical and temporary.

AT THE TIME IT DIDN'T LOOK LIKE I was ever going to see, much less get to do, her, and I couldn't shake the image of her servicing those fat cats, or worse, Rita's fat cat. Even though those images were just made up by me, the fact that they were there was symbolic of the fact that the new girl in payable wasn't where she was supposed to be, in payable, where I could get a look at her.

It went that way all afternoon, with me finding reasons to check into payable and going back to my desk disappointed. Finally, KC powered down and collected his things—jacket, ballcap, briefcase. He actually wears a ballcap and carries a briefcase.

"Five already?" I said.

He didn't answer.

"KC," I said.

"I'm not gonna bother talking to anyone who thinks the new girl in payable is a dog," KC said.

He didn't look up until he'd finished saying it, and when he did, he actually looked sad from that angle, puppy-eyed, in puppy love with a dog. Except he always looks puppy-eyed from that angle because his face is puffy and jowly. And of course, the new girl in payable wasn't a dog.

"I don't really think she's a dog," I said.

"Then why'd you say it?" he said.

I wasn't quick enough coming up with an answer.

"You still haven't seen her," he said, and when my expression confirmed it against my will, he collapsed in laughter, almost fell out of his chair.

It wasn't that funny.

"What's so funny?" I said.

He collected himself and collected his things again, got up to go.

"I'm going," he said.

He tried to brush past me but I held out an arm, didn't really use force to stop him, just signaled my willingness to do so.

"KC," I said. "What's with the new girl?"

He laughed again. Chuckled, I mean. I let my arm drop to my side.

"Figure it out for yourself, *Knight Rider*," he said, and got by me.

I stood with my back to him, glaring at his empty cubicle.

"Don't call me that," I said.

"Fine, Michael," he said in this half-robot, half-British accent that was meant to sound like the way Knight Rider's car talked.

I turned to look at him. He'd stopped at the corner, waiting for it.

"Mike," I said. "Mike Long."

"You wanna know the thing about the new girl, Mike Long?" he said.

Before I had the chance to answer he had his hands up at his shoulders. He extended them out as far as he could and brought them back to his ribs having mimed a perfect parabola.

I don't even like big breasts. I mean, I'm not against them, but they aren't kinky black hair if that makes any sense. And besides, any woman with breasts as big as KC had outlined would have trouble standing straight. I was about to tell him that when he cracked up again, waved his arm to say you're hopeless, and disappeared around the corner. But I didn't feel hopeless at all. I felt vindicated.

Breasts. Big ones. They were the exact thing to make an entire local branch of a major corporation act like idiots for a full business day, and now everything made sense, because I was immune to them, in fact, repulsed if there was any hint they were fake, just another case of my being the odd man out.

I started to gather my own things, but I felt guilty I hadn't gotten anything accomplished all day. Then I remembered what I'd been writing when it all started. I brought up my browser, and the email was right there where I'd left it, still unsent.

That morning, Ms. Miles, our boss, had sent a message to the entire office asking us to welcome April Curtis to the organization. It said she would be working in payable and that we should do whatever we could to help her out as she adjusted to her new position. I had hit reply all and written:

> Hi, April,
>
> Welcome to the family! Please let me know if there's anything I can do to help as you adjust to your new position.
>
> Sincerely,
>
> Mike Long

I'd been going for a combination of personable (hi, family) and professional (please, sincerely), because I'd just been thinking of her as another new hire. I mean, all I knew about her was that her name was April Curtis. That name sounded totally uninteresting, ordinary. I know there's no official, you know, biological connection between names and their people, but think about it—when was the last time you met a real knockout whose parents had named her after a month. Mae West, maybe, but that's spelled wrong.

I decided that, given the events of the day and what I'd learned about her, I needed to be much more formal and much more specific, so I deleted what I had, and wrote:

> Ms. Curtis,
>
> Congratulations and welcome. Perhaps we should meet for coffee in the next few days so that I can explain to you the difference between a post-it note and a paperclip if it's not too late already.
>
> Yours,
>
> Mike Long

I hit send. I put the computer to sleep. I headed down the hall feeling like I'd really accomplished something on Monday.

I stopped into payable on the way out. As I'd suspected—no one there. I walked past the empty reception desk and shut off the lights. Out by the elevators, I told myself to ignore the women's room altogether. I pressed the arrow down and the door opened right away for once.

II

I JUST REALIZED THAT IT'S ALREADY Tuesday. Actually, it's still, technically, Monday, but that's another Monday, not the week I'm apologizing for. In any case, now I've apologized for Monday, that is, the Monday that concerns us (i.e., not today), and, of course, only the part of the Monday that concerns us that concerns us. In other words, the business day. I mean, I could tell you that I went home and futzed around online and finally had a couple of glasses of wine before bed, but anything more would probably get in the way, and frankly, is none of your business.

So it's Tuesday and I haven't told you anything about myself, not, again, that it's any of your business. But it might give you a better sense of where I'm coming from. I'm extending it as a courtesy, a courtesy that could work to my advantage by helping you see things from my perspective.

Tuesday is as good a day as any to do this. Better, actually, because nothing relevant to the apology happened on Tuesday, unless you're some kind of Buddhist monk, or cabalist or something, and you think that nothing is something. So I'll give you a quick rundown of Tuesday in case Eastern mysticism is your thing.

Dateline Tuesday. Nothing happened but not in an existential way. Office Manager Mike Long still did not see the new girl in payable. Kit Carson the computer guy made a number of disgusting comments about her to show his appreciation and insisted he had crossed paths with her several times in the course of business. He also directed a few obnoxious comments toward Mr. Long, but there really was no chemistry between them that day. By the time he went home, Long was starting to doubt the new girl in payable existed, and it occurred to him that she could be a prank the entire office was playing on him. This idea caused much tossing and turning as he lay in bed, and he had to take a double dose of Nyquil to fall asleep (not that it's any of the reader's business).

Now on to the real business of Tuesday, which is everything that happened to me before Tuesday.

My name is Mike Long, though I wasn't born that way. I was born in a small town right here in this great state. My father was a failed novelist, which is probably where I got my way with words, so he had to become an English teacher. My mother owned a stationery shop, which is probably where I got my way with office supplies and is definitely where I got this stationery I am writing on. I have it shipped to me under my new name, a way to stay connected even if she won't talk to me.

Before I was done growing up something happened that I don't feel like writing about right now because I'll have to write about it again soon enough anyway. For now I'll just say that it was big, almost witness protection big, and that was when my name got changed.

But because my name got changed there was no record of my existence before my senior year of high school, and so I had to change my dream of going somewhere ivy, which had been the plan all along, and I ended up at a state school. I bet you can guess what I majored in based on certain hints I've been dropping in this apology. ("Apology" was another hint, by the way, probably gratuitous by now.) That's right—philosophy. I did pretty good at it, too. Wrote my thesis on some parallels I saw between Hegel's theory of absolute spirit, and particularly his notion of world historical individuals, and a certain television show from the 80s about a vigilante who wore a Member's Only jacket and drove a talking Pontiac.

Now I bet you're wondering how a philosopher like me ended up in office management. Well, it's kind of a funny story, but more like an anecdote. A funny anecdote.

When I was a senior in college, I had planned to apply to grad school and probably would have, but my advisor wouldn't write me a recommendation. So, like anybody in my situation, I went to the university's spring employment fair and interviewed for a job with a middle-aged lady in a powder blue powersuit. The next week, I got a call asking if I could come in to interview for a position someone thought I might be suited for, and the next day I managed to take the bus to the city and make it through a whole interview without looking inappropriate or saying anything bad. A week later I was offered the job. I accepted immediately, and started a month after that. That was something over six years ago.

But that isn't the end of the story of me until last Tuesday. There was my career, for example, which is the real subject of this apology, and one other thing, the thing about me and Kit Carson and why we have the relationship we have.

As you might have noticed, the Apollo Creed of Office Suite and I got off on the wrong foot, so after the ChlorAmmo thing blew over, I started looking for ways to smooth things out. One afternoon, his cellphone went off. I saw my chance and took it.

KC was a gadget-geek. It came with the profession. He seemed to have a different ringtone every couple of days. Most of them were just weak-speaker warbled versions of modern rock songs that blended into each other, snippets from tales of tough men with raspy voices losing lurv in a burd wur.

But that day it was different, a tune near and dear to my heart, so familiar I named it in about two staccato stabs. It was the theme song from the same old television show I'd done my thesis on.

KC answered, said, "yo," listened, said, "that sucks," then, "later dog," and his conversation was over, the phone back in his front pocket.

"They used to call me Knight Rider back home," I said.

"So?" he said.

"Don't you think it's interesting?" I said, "Your ringtone? My nickname? And your name is Kit, like the talking car?"

"My name's Kit Carson," he said. "I'm named after Kit Carson."

To me, Kit Carson was just a vague memory of a syndicated TV show about a vigilante who was friends with a talking Mexican. I'd seen maybe a few episodes on cable when I was a kid, about thirty years after its original run.

"The TV show?" I said.

"The mountain man," he said.

This wasn't getting me anywhere.

"Forget about it," I said.

"I'm gonna call you Knight Rider," he said.

That was when I realized I'd made a mistake. I'd been so eager to find some common ground with KC that I hadn't thought what it could lead to. I didn't need anybody digging into my past as Knight Rider.

"KC," I said, "keep the Knight Rider thing between us?" I said.

"Why?" he said. "You call me KC when that's not *my* real name."

"Keep it between us, Kit?"

He shrugged, smiled, pointed at his phone, said, "That was my boy. He just canceled on me."

I should have known that if it seemed too easy, it was.

"Sorry," I said.

"You wanna go have a beer and watch the game?" he said.

I didn't know what game he was talking about, but I figured it would help conceal my secret identity and I didn't have anything better to do. I never had anything better to do, so I went.

We ended up at an Applebee's near the office, and KC drank seven pints to my two before the game even started. It turned out it was football, which is why I remember it was a Monday night. When the national anthem came on, KC started throwing a fit in this weird pirate voice, arrghing about how our team was going to lose, because they lose every time a white girl sings it, because it makes them play white, and even though he didn't manage to cause much of a scene—the place was crowded, and our fans are rowdy enough to cover up most any scene you try to cause—I was out of there before kickoff.

But I was pretty sure we were friends by then, confident I didn't have to worry about anyone learning my old name. The next morning I found out I was wrong. He came in with a yell-whisper, just like he had after the ChlorAmmo.

"I got a DUI last night," he said, "and it's your fault, Knight Rider."

"Kit," I said, "I asked you to call me Mike."

"My license is gonna be suspended for six months," he said.

"You were drunk," I said. "I can't do anything about that."

"Yes you can," he said.

It turned out I could. I could show up at his place every Saturday morning for the next six months, in a car share because KC said if he couldn't drive his Trans Am, no one could, and chauffeur his ass around. I went along with it to protect my identity.

KC lived out in the 'burbs, one of the ones you see listed on commuter train schedules but can't quite be sure exists. I pulled up in front of his house early, but he was already waiting. He threw a heavy duffel bag into the back and flopped down in the passenger seat like my existence was an imposition. I wondered what he had planned for the first day.

"Where to?" I said.

The Hercules of Hardware guided me to a strip mall a few suburbs from his, and we parked in front of a gym. Inside, mats covered the entire floor of the large, open space, and the place smelled like air conditioning and sweat. I took a seat in the waiting area, and KC went into the locker room. When he emerged, there were a dozen of him, or at least it looked that way—twelve chubby, middle-aged men in sweatpants. There was some variation in T-shirts (power metal, professional wrestling promotion), a surprising array of balding patterns, and goatee-sculpture ranging from conservative to whimsical, but there was very little else to distinguish one from another. I was pretty sure KC was the one with the Coors logo plastered across his chest.

Another man emerged from what looked like a small office in the back corner. I figured him for the coach or trainer or whatever you call it. The men paired off, circled each other, took a couple of swings apiece, and then, almost in unison, embraced, dropped to the floor, and humped each other, occasionally flopping around so that the man on the bottom could be on top and vice versa. The man from the office walked around giving each pair encouragement and suggestions, I guess, until he announced that it was time to start over. The men regrouped, sometimes switched partners, and did the whole thing over again and again until it was time to hit the showers.

Afterward, KC and I went dutch to the Outback Steakhouse in the same strip mall.

"How'd I look out there?" he said.

The way he said it, it sounded like he knew it was something to be ashamed of, not necessarily the Mixed Martial Arts or the homoeroticism of it, or even his individual performance. He seemed to be ashamed that the class was a group of grown men that didn't already know how to snap someone's neck with a leglock, that they hadn't been born with the knowledge, or demonstrated the ability at their baptisms or confirmations.

"I'm not sure I understand the game," I said.

"It's not a game," he said. "It's a martial art. Actually several martial arts."

"What's the point?" I said.

"It's a lot like life," he said. "There are strength guys and strategy guys."

I wanted to ask which one he considered himself, but he'd already moved on to tales of the incredible battles that had been fought on the very mats on which I'd watched him roll around that morning. I looked forward to seeing some of these battles, because they would have to be more entertaining than the foreplay I'd just witnessed.

It was a month of Mixed Martial Arts practices and deep-fried lunches before I realized that the foreplay *was* the battle, at least in that gym, and the mozzarella sticks and potato skins were the victory celebrations or the consolations of defeat. We didn't always go to Outback—there was a Ruby Tuesday as well, a Friendly's, an Olive Garden after, according to KC, a particularly epic campaign—but the struggle always looked more or less the same to me. Still, over time I started to be able to tell the men apart, and as their identities came into focus, so did their stories. The man with the blond ponytail was jealous of the attention the man with the Bugs Bunny tattoo showed to the man with the brown ponytail. The man who owned at least six Marlboro shirts seemed to hate and love the man who was missing the last two fingers of his right hand in equal measure. No one seemed to feel any particular way toward KC, so I ignored him, knowing that I'd get the mythologized version of whatever he'd done at Pizza Hut later. Aside from his scenes, I was pretty wrapped up in the whole soap opera, but not enough to keep going after my sentence was up.

As I dropped him off one Saturday, I said: "So this should be it, huh?"

"It should be what?" he said.

"It's been six months," I said.

I couldn't decide if he still wanted company or just revenge, or if there was even a difference.

"I'd kind of started thinking of you as my cheering section," he said.

"I'm a lover, not a fighter," I said.

It seemed as though the same could be said of any man in the class.

"Or my manager," he said. "Like if I ever went pro."

I knew enough to know he was never going pro.

"I was just keeping you company until your suspension was over," I said.

"Fine, Knight Rider," he said, and slammed the door.

I don't know which made me angriest—when he went back to calling me Knight Rider, when I overheard him telling Edward that the guys in his MMA class were totally creeped out by the way I sat there staring at them and he didn't know why I insisted on driving out to watch every weekend, or when I found out he'd never gotten that DUI in the first place. Probably the Knight Rider thing. The other stuff mostly made me sad.

THAT PRETTY MUCH BRINGS US UP to last Tuesday, but I worry you'll think I'm trying to avoid telling you anything about Tuesday, so I will tell you something about Tuesday that has absolutely no meaning so you'll know how meaningless it was.

On Tuesday I took a late lunch because I thought maybe if I stopped into payable after everyone else was back I might see the new girl, but of course all I saw was Edward and everyone else, everyone but the new girl. So I went down to the food court because I figured the crowd would have thinned out by then and it had. I got a sandwich from Subway and sat down not far from there. There was no one sitting within five tables of me. And then suddenly a guy came along. In his dusty work boots and tough grubby jeans, he looked like one of the construction workers from the site across the street. He stopped at the table right in front of me and sat down facing me. He placed his sandwich in front of him and started swiping at the wrapping like his hands were paws, like he refused to use his fingers as fingers. He spread the wrapper to each side of the sandwich with the axe handles of his fists and stared at his meal like there was a shaft of light shining down on it from the sky, which there was not, and you can't see the sky from the mezzanine floor of a skyscraper. Then he raised his hands a little and finally used his fingers, wriggling them like oh-this-is-going-to-be-a-delectable-experience, and as if that was not enough his eyes popped and his head wobbled from side to side to say what-have-we-here when we know very well it's a skimpy sandwich. For a second I felt like I was in a commercial about food that would satisfy the hungriest man. He took a bite and his face almost moaned how decadent and sinful his sandwich was and did the same thing for each bite I saw after that. My sandwich was not like that at all.

To tell the truth it was disgusting, and so I left in disgust. And that happened on Tuesday.

Wednesday

You might have noticed that I've been organizing my apology by day. To that end, I've decided, starting today, to head each day with its proper title, for ease of reference. Hence the big bold Wednesday on the preceding page.

Wednesday then. I was still groggy when I got into work, because of the aforementioned tossing and turning and Nyquil. Asleep on my feet. So I wasn't surprised at first when I got to my desk and saw Edward and KC conferring around KC's desk in conspiratorial fashion. I sat down in my chair and woke my computer up. But as my computer woke up so did I, and I started to register the strangeness of what I'd seen. The strangeness was this: I had never seen Edward outside of payable, much less at KC's desk.

I looked back at them—the slowest doubletake in office history—and caught Edward stealing a glance at me. Edward, who's never in on anything, who can't hide even the most subtle emotion, who now seemed to think he could hide the all-too-obvious—that they were talking about me.

Edward knew I'd caught him, and I could see he was nervous. More nervous than usual. KC hadn't noticed. He was still going on about whatever he'd been going on about. He pointed in my direction dismissively, without looking, and I saw Edward wince. Then KC did the huge breasts gesture again and cracked himself up, but quietly. Before he had composed himself I was standing over him, beside Edward, and Edward was already doing the body language of it-was-nice-catching-up-with-you-but-now-I-better-get-back-to-my-desk.

KC, on the other hand, looked up and met my eyes as though he'd expected to find me there, which was about the last thing I'd expected from him at that moment. I also didn't expect him to address me so casually, with no trace of the usual aggression.

"How's it going, Mike?" he said.

Believe me when I tell you he had said those words in that tone exactly zero times before, ever.

"We were just talking about the new girl in payable," he said. "Definitely the hottest girl that ever worked here. Right, Edward?"

"Yeah," said Edward.

He nodded, at least I think he was nodding. It might have just been a tremor.

KC kept staring at him like he'd expected something else, a more affirmative action. It was almost gratifying to see his stare get more insistent. Sweat beaded on Edward's forehead and a vein popped from his temple. I was thinking he might pass out when his mouth dropped open and "What about you, Mike?" practically fell out. It barely even sounded like words, and it was obvious KC had put him up to mumbling them.

"Still haven't seen her," I said.

Edward seemed relieved.

"It was nice catching up with you guys, but now I've got to get back to my desk," he said.

He was gone before we had a chance to say goodbye.

"You still haven't seen her?" KC said.

I shook my head no.

"Seriously," he said, "the hottest who's ever worked here."

I wanted to tell him that meant nothing to me. Up until then I hadn't seen anyone at all attractive in the office. Maybe the woman who'd hired me—the one in the powder blue powersuit—but she was a little old and I'd never seen her again, anyway.

"She was down in payable when I got in," said KC. "Like ten minutes ago."

I almost smacked myself. I'd been so groggy that I forgot to look into payable as I passed. I dropped all pretense to disinterest right then and there. I turned and bolted down the hall without another word.

Everyone in payable was in payable when I got there, everyone except for the new girl. I did a quick look around to make sure, and then went straight for Edward. He was just settling into his chair, his mug trembling at his lips when I reached him.

"Edward," I said.

He jumped and some of his coffee jumped the mug, landed in his lap. Not enough to burn him, just enough to embarrass him and maybe leave an all-day stain on his lighter-than-standard khakis. But then he tried to wipe it off with the hand that held the mug, and fresh coffee scalded his lap and he yelped.

"Edward," I said like a command, "where's the new girl?"

Edward was still yelping and the rest of payable was up now, swarming and swooping. Two of them, a man and a woman, shoved past me from opposite sides, each with a pile of napkins at the end of an outstretched arm. One of them dove for his lap while the other went straight for the puddle around the mug on Edward's desk, sopping up spilled coffee, like they'd practiced for precisely this moment. Soon Edward's yelps had shriveled to soft moans, and the whole department was surrounding him, his desk, surrounding me. I didn't dare to look at them, focused instead on the tears of that clown Edward.

"What did I do?" he moaned, slobbered, "what did I ever do?"

"You spilled your coffee. That's what you did," I said.

I felt some vaguely threatening nudges in my ribs and back and finally looked around, met my implicit accusers with a stare. I'd said it matter-of-factly, without a hint of malice, just an observation, so I felt justified in adding, for their sake and the sake of my convictions: "That's what he did."

Cindy tried to give me this you-just-don't-get-it look, but she has one of those mouths that makes every expression look dumb, so it didn't come off right. Fong, the master of righteous indignation, said, sputtered, "Have a little sympathy. The man's in pain," but it just looked weird. I couldn't read his body language because he looked disembodied. All I could see was his head hovering over Cindy's shoulder.

You could see how that could be funny, right? I tried to stifle the laugh but my hand couldn't catch it.

"It's not funny," Fong said, holier now than Jesus himself.

My hand had reached my mouth by then, but the laughs were coming hard and fast and would not be contained.

"You're sick," said Cindy, "laughing at a burn victim."

At first that seemed even funnier than Fong's floating head because Cindy's mouth is too dumb to get even indignation—much less righteousness—right, and I laughed even harder. But then my brain started to absorb what she'd said and I realized I hadn't taken a moment to soberly consider Edward's condition, and also that I'd pretty much forgotten him.

I looked at Edward. Edward looked fine, looked like he was maybe even enjoying the attention, not from most of us, who were pretty much fixated on me, who was not enjoying himself at all by then, but from Karen, who, as I've implied by my blanket description of all women in office history, was not attractive, but who was still wiping his lap, her napkins frayed and crumbling on his crotch. When she noticed us all staring she stopped, stood up straight.

I wished ChlorAmmo existed.

"Are you okay, Edward?" I said.

"I'm fine," said Edward.

Everybody finally got bored and went back to their cubicles. Once we were left alone-ish, Edward locked his fingers behind his head, elbows making butterfly wings in the air to either side, relaxed for real.

"What can I do for you?" he said.

"I'm looking for the new girl," I said.

I said it like an accusation, like I knew he was hiding her in his desk.

"The new girl," said Edward, like a fact.

"The new girl," I said.

"The new *woman*," he said in stone.

Whatever, Edward.

"Where is the new woman!" I yelled, loud enough, I know now, to be heard all the way down the hall.

It made Edward jump again, but fortunately he didn't have any coffee left to spill. Or unfortunately. I can't decide anymore.

"She went to get us some coffee," he said.

"But you already *had* coffee," I said.

"Edward got the last cup," Fong said from behind me.

"I spilled it," Edward said.

"Now Edward needs a cup, too," said Karen. "I'll call her," she said.

"I already did," said Cindy. "She was halfway here, but she said no problem she'd go back and get Edward a cup. Such an angel."

I rushed over to Cindy's cube, looked over the divider as Karen said: "Edward deserves it after what he's been through," as if he'd been through anything. Cindy was sitting there, her hand still on the receiver, looking satisfied. Satisfied and dumb.

"I want coffee, too," I said.

Cindy looked up, surprised to see me standing over her. She probably would have spilled her coffee if she'd had any, but as she registered me and then what I'd said, her expression went from surprise to disdain.

"How many arms do you think she has?" she said.

It was unsettling to see how well her dumb mouth could do how-dumb-can-you-be? and I never wanted to see it again. I did a quick look around the office, just to double-check, because I was already pretty sure there were six people in there not including me, and there were. I looked back to Cindy before I said: "Well let's see. There are six of you here, so six. Unless she's getting one for herself. Six or seven arms," I said.

Cindy did the same expression again, but I rendered it ineffective, at least to myself, with the situational irony of knowing I was being ironic.

"Jesus, Mike," she said, and I successfully stifled the laugh so I could listen to her go on. "They have these things called trays? And the trays carry four cups each?"

I was about to ask if she was asking me or telling, but I know that my irony is not always appreciated, and now I wanted something from her.

“Okay,” I said, “assuming she can carry one tray with each hand, that equals eight cups of coffee. There are seven of you including her and Edward, which leaves room for one, which could be mine.”

“Could have been yours,” Karen said from behind me. I turned to catch her drift. “We wouldn’t be vindictive enough to penalize you from having one of your own if you were really sorry.”

“Which we’re not sure you are,” said Fong, his self-righteous head hovering above his partition.

“But it doesn’t matter, anyway,” said Karen. “We already promised one to Kit Carson.”

I hadn’t heard the actual name in so long that it sounded nostalgic, like a sepia-toned rerun. I had to say it over and over in my head just to make the connection, and still it didn’t seem right.

“Kit Carson?” I said. “You mean KC?”

“Whatever,” said Cindy.

I didn’t even need to look back at her to prove that her face could no longer faze me.

“I’m going,” I said.

“Good,” said Karen, but it fell on my deaf back, because I was already mostly out of payable, down the hall in spirit, certain that someone would have to deliver KC’s coffee to our part of the office, and who better than the new girl? Such an angel.

"**What were you yelling about?**" KC said when I got back to my desk, but I didn't answer, because I was already distracted, had been distracted since halfway down the hall by the folder in my inbox. Distracted because the folder was a shade of green brighter than any I'd ever seen, which is odd because as office manager I get, got, paid to know my office products, including color scales, and because my inbox was almost always empty.

The folder contained a photocopy of the new girl's HR file.

Her résumé was as dull as her name. Nothing too attractive about her education—state school like me but not the same one, majored in French, decent GPA. Her work history was pretty boring, unless you were me, or someone else who grew up in the same town as I did, because at the bottom of the page I got to the beginning of her career and found that she'd started out in the town I grew up in, and not just the same town, but my mother's stationery shop.

My mother never had more than one or two employees at a time, after school and weekend type stuff. I did the math and this April Curtis was claiming to have worked for my mother during my senior year of high school and for two years after, specifically beginning just after the big thing happened that I still don't feel like talking about. I supposed it was possible my mother had had an employee I'd never heard of after I left—it wasn't like she would answer my calls after my father and I "disappeared." But where would this April Curtis have come from? It wasn't such a big town, and there were no April Curtises there *before* I left. Meaning, I couldn't really believe she was who she said she was or that she had done what she said she'd done.

I started to doubt my own memory. Maybe there *had* been an April Curtis. But no, there had not.

"What you got there?" said KC.

I snapped the folder shut.

"Nothing," I said.

KC shrugged and took a sip of coffee. If I'd been thinking straight I would have been suspicious about his lack of curiosity—when did KC ever let anything go with a shrug?—but I wasn't thinking straight. I was doubting myself and easily swayed and KC was sipping from a cup of fresh, hot coffee.

"Where'd you get the coffee?" I said.

He pulled the paper cup from his lips and appraised it as though I'd asked him where the beans were from.

"This?" he said. "The new girl in payable."

"April Curtis?" I said.

"Is that her name?" he said. "Never got it. Too busy paying attention to—"

He brought the hand that wasn't holding the coffee up to his shoulder to do the huge breast thing again, but I didn't let him finish.

"I know," I said.

"You've seen her?" he said.

"Yeah," I said. I saw KC glance toward the file and kind of slid it behind my back. "Can I borrow your car tonight?" I said.

He said no.

Before I write another word about this, I have to tell you something I left out of Tuesday, which means I admit to leaving something out of Tuesday. It's not directly relevant to the apology, but it goes to my mindstate, and so I'll include it, possibly against my better judgment and wishes. So,

A Secret Tuesday in the Middle of Wednesday

So much for ease of reference.

It was late on Tuesday afternoon, and I was on my way back from popping into payable again—of course she wasn't there—and passing by receivable when somebody yelled out, "He's jumping!" and everybody else shrieked. I ran into processing and all I caught through the window was an earth-toned blur dropping past steel girders across the street.

Everyone in the office was crowded against the glass. The shrieks had been shocked into silence by whatever had happened.

"What happened," I asked, as gently as I could.

No one answered and so I asked again. When I still got no reaction, I decided to go back to my end and see what KC thought.

I was running up the hall when I slammed into KC, knocked him on his ass. He barely had time to get a hand behind him to break his fall, but he was up as fast as he'd dropped.

"What the fuck?" he said, looking down at the camera dangling by its strap from his neck, which must have been why he hadn't seen me coming in the first place.

"Something happened down there," I said.

"Where do you think I was going?" he said.

"Did somebody jump?" I said.

"You wanna come watch me take pictures?" he said, still distracted by the viewfinder.

I heard the first sirens in the distance and some weird monotone moans coming from processing and maybe even receivable. I wanted to know what had happened, but not up close and personal.

"I gotta get to my desk," I said.

By the time KC came back, now smiling at the viewfinder on his camera, I'd been sitting at my desk for twenty minutes, near catatonic, just staring straight ahead. KC stopped in front of me, shoved the camera in front of my face, and said: "Check this out."

I didn't get a good look at it. The screen was tiny and the resolution low and I didn't look long. To tell the truth it reminded me of spaghetti, but not the good kind. The kind that comes in a can. But in that one brief glance before I pushed the camera away and told KC he was sick, I thought I saw something in that organic red mess. I thought I could make out a pair of work boots stretching out like the splatter-patterns toward the north side of the street. So I needed to see it again.

I couldn't think of a good way to take back what I'd said, so I said, "Let me see that again?"

"I thought I was sick," said KC.

"I'm sorry," I said, "just let me see."

"What's the magic word?" he said.

"Please let me see the picture, Mr. Carson," I said, maybe a little too sarcastically.

"Fuck you, dude," he said, and walked away, to show the splatter-porn to someone else I guess.

Back to Wednesday

You can see why I tried to leave that out. And then why I tried to bury it in a secret Tuesday in the middle of Wednesday. But it wouldn't stay there. It followed me all the way through the Tuesday night tossing and turning that required Nyquil, through Wednesday morning's grogginess, and up to my Wednesday afternoon desktop, the one on my computer, I mean. I woke it back up after shoving April Curtis's file to the bottom of my bottom-most desk drawer, and there it was, the picture KC had shown me the day before, but blown up and pixilated and plastered across my screen.

It wasn't too traumatic at first because the stretching abstracted it, but then I saw what I'd thought were boots, and they were definitely boots, despite the distortion. As I continued to stare down at the screen, I noticed, a little closer to the center, what might have been denim, blue jeans soaked near purple in blood. I know that most construction workers wear blue jeans and boots, and that the occasional construction site accident, even a fatal one, is inevitable if usually avoidable, but I couldn't shake the sense that the mess had been the man I'd seen in the food court Tuesday, and that his fall could not have been accidental, because he was a man's man, and men's men don't die by accident.

Knowing that people don't often make the decision to kill themselves on the spur of the moment, I had to ask myself how I could have missed noticing that the man had been in pain, that the way he'd eaten his sandwich was in fact an advertisement, a performance, a denial of the pain he was in, and I wondered if his last meal had actually brought him any pleasure, or if it had disappointed him as it had disappointed and disgusted me, and I wondered if that disappointment—that Subway had lied to him, that even the manliest sandwich could not give his life meaning—was the final straw or just part of a pattern, and if a pattern, how were things at work? Was the environment toxic or just not what he'd hoped for? Had he imagined, as a boy, building a new world, brick by brick and rivet by rivet, only to end up risking his life daily, high up on steel girders in bitter winds, to finish the office of a man who makes a hundred times what he does just sitting on his ass? Or had his coworkers driven him to it, with some myth, maybe, about a coworker who didn't really exist? Because that was exactly how I had felt for the past two days, but was only just then ready to admit. I wasn't managing office for truth, justice, and the American way; I was managing office for a tiny little branch of a huge corporation. And April Curtis's convenient disappearances and bright green file and probably bullshit connection to my mother's stationery business seemed like more than another tedious prank. In other words, think of the man who jumped as a metaphor for me, because that was where I was headed if I didn't do something soon.

So I did something. I clicked the browser icon where the mess's head would have been and reserved a Civic, black, from the carshare for ten that night. Then I crawled under my desk and went to sleep and stayed there all the way to the proverbial closing bell and beyond.

Thursday

THERE'S SOMETHING I NEED TO TELL you before I get started on Thursday. It's that stalking implies an interest. The extent of my interest to that point had been non-interest, or maybe disinterest, in the old judicial, you know, philosophical sense. Ergo, you can trust me not to have been a stalker, never to have stalked, even when appearances might suggest otherwise, because even if appearances suggest stalking, you have to consider the possibility that the disinterested behavior of the apparition is scientific, and you wouldn't call Einstein a stalker, would you? Except he did all of his experiments in his head. So that other scientist then. The one whose bladder exploded.

Besides, I'm an office manager, or I was at that point, and how many office managers are toothless and stubbled and drink about a case of beer in their pickups while staring up at the new girl's window to see if she'll change into her pajamas in front of that window? Because you don't have to watch as many police procedurals as I do to know that that's exactly how stalkers stalk and what they look like when they do it, and you only need to try doing it once, even if you have all of your teeth and have to borrow, say, a Civic from the carshare because the Prince of Programmers won't let you borrow his Trans Am, to know that it would be damn near impossible to maintain the stalker lifestyle and an office job.

So Thursday started where Wednesday left off—at the stroke of midnight. It found me in a black Civic outside April Curtis's apartment building.

I don't remember much from the beginning of Wednesday's nap to that moment, because, to be honest, and you must realize now that that's what this is about—honesty—honestly, I wasn't conscious for much of it.

I'd awoken beneath my desk feeling surprisingly refreshed for the first time that week. The office was dark, but I didn't have a good sense of what time it was. I guess no one had noticed me sleeping down there because no one had bothered to wake me up, and there were no signs anyone had played any pranks on me, which you know would have happened if KC had found me asleep on the office floor. There was nothing but a little puddle of drool on the short-pile carpet. I couldn't actually see it in the dark, but I could feel the cold damp against my cheek.

I crawled out from under my desk and looked around the office. I recognized its shapes and shadows against the yellow-pink city lights peeping through the back windows, but it was all different than I was used to. I mean that in a good way.

A glance at the clock on the wall told me it was 10:30 p.m. Still technically Wednesday, but that's hardly relevant.

I'd had some time to cool off, and my plan seemed a little crazy by then, but I sat down at my desk and woke up my computer. While I waited for it to warm up, I rummaged through my bottom drawer and pulled out April Curtis's HR file. Before I even had it in front of the now humming computer, I could sense it glowing kryptonite green.

The address of her cover letter told me she lived nearby. Easy walking distance. Also within easy walking distance of my apartment which is very close to the office. But foot patrol wasn't an option because it was cold out and because I would be too conspicuous standing on the sidewalk staring up at her building all night long.

It was already a few hours past my reservation for the car, but the website said it was sitting right where it was supposed to be, in a lot closer to my place than the office, but equidistant between my place and April Curtis's. I'd planned to go home first. I didn't have time to do that now.

I shut off my computer. The office was dark pink but the hallway was black, so I inched along the wall until I saw the light from the elevator banks. The elevator seemed almost to have been waiting for me. It took me right down. I nodded to the security guard as casually as I could on my way out.

Something crunched beneath my feet as I walked past the entrance to the office parking garage. I took it for rock salt but couldn't see whatever it was. I didn't remember any ice or snow in the forecast—it was a little too early in the season for that—but figured maybe management was being better safe than sorry. The wind gusted and I heard something flap like thunder in a high school play and glanced across the street. It was a banner, spraypaint on a sheet, reading "We'll miss you, Mitch." It dangled from between two steel girders on the construction site. A memorial to their fallen colleague, I guessed. I walked on, not wanting to think about it, not wanting that to be me.

I stopped at the store on the corner and grabbed a six pack of beer. I knew I was supposed to get something shitty, Coors or Bud or something, but I couldn't stomach the idea and got the sweet kind, wheat, instead.

It seemed like it had gotten colder in the minute or so I'd been inside, the wind harder and sharper, so I picked up speed and was sitting in the lot fifteen minutes later, numb and steaming the windows, waiting for the car to warm up.

Five minutes after that I pulled up in front of April Curtis's building.

It was a big, turn-of-the-century brownstone with cute little flower plots to either side of the stoop. I realized as I pulled up in front of it that I hadn't considered whether her apartment faced front or rear. The building was large enough that there were maybe four units on each floor. She lived in apartment 3B, which meant she lived on the third floor, but whether I could see it from the street was unclear. I looked up to the third story. There was a light on in one of the four windows. I hoped it was hers since nothing was going on in any of the others.

I cut the engine, reached into the bag on the seat beside me, and pulled out a beer. When I tried to twist it open the cap dug into my palm. I untucked my shirt and put it over the top, tried again to twist.

It wasn't a twist-off, and I didn't have a bottle opener. I crammed the bottle back into the bag.

I craned my neck up toward the third floor. I couldn't see enough from that position, so I shifted sideways, my back to the driver's side door, and kind of slumped down, propping my legs up on the beer bag. With my chin pressed against my chest I could see about half of the third story window. There were no signs of life. All I could think of was how uncomfortable I was, and to tell the truth, the position must have been cutting off my oxygen supply because I started to feel tired and soon I was nodding off.

I snapped out of it, sat upright, and weighed my options, decided I might as well get out and stretch my legs, because if I didn't, I wouldn't see anything and the night would be a complete waste.

I got out and stretched my legs. It was colder still. I huddled and made for a stoop across the street where I figured I'd have a good view of the window and hoped I'd be taken for a vagrant by any passerby. The stoop was cold against my ass and the wind was strong and I wished I had a cup of coffee or a churchkey so that at least I could get oblivious with beer.

I cursed myself for that and all my other failures, but as I did, I caught a movement in the third-floor window. I focused just in time to see a cat slink out of view. A few seconds after that a huge mass moved in from the right, and soon it had filled the whole frame. Whatever it was *did* have huge breasts, but she had huge everything else too, part for part the size at least of Rita. I tried to imagine two women that size doing whatever I'd imagined Rita and April doing in a single bathroom stall and realized it was impossible, knew they could never fit. I tried to imagine the whole office getting so worked up over some monstrosity simply because her breasts were slightly more monstrous proportionally, and hoped, for the sake of modern masculinity, that it wasn't the case. I knew it couldn't be, or else all the guys would have been sweating Rita all along, and they hadn't.

There were two possibilities: Either the woman in the window wasn't April Curtis, or I was the victim of an elaborate but stupid prank. The stupid part sounded about right, but I doubted KC's ability to orchestrate the elaboration. Either way the night was a bust, no pun intended. But I hoped it was the former. Otherwise the whole week to that point had been pointless too.

I was ready to leave, about to get up and go back to the car, when the woman in the window lifted an arm. For a second I thought I'd been caught. It looked like she was waving at me. I couldn't make out her face to confirm because she was backlit. Then she raised her other hand to the same height and I knew she had no idea I was there. It became even clearer when she brought both hands to her collar and pulled up on her shirt.

It must have been made of some heavy fabric because it pulled the tips, if you could call them tips, of those enormous breasts upward, so that I saw her belly first, and the undersides of the tits, and then, when her head was mostly covered by the shirt, the breasts dropped heavy from the hem, falling fast and slapping her gut. Even in the shadows, I saw the waves pass through her flesh. As things settled, my eyes were directed downward as though the breasts were arrows, dark areolas the size of small saucers aimed at the belly button they wobbled indifferently above.

I am not a pervert, but I could not get up just then because my pants were too tight, and I couldn't look away because where else was there to look? Where were those arrows pointing? They were pointing precisely nowhere. There was no point to those tits. But they rose again slightly as the woman in the window lifted her arm until it reached a cord in the upper right hand corner and the blinds came down, leaving the woman a silhouette on a screen, and then the arm came down. A minute later the woman walked away from the window and it seemed to brighten drastically without all of that bulk blocking the light. Then suddenly the light itself was gone and the whole façade of the building was dark.

It was a few minutes still before I could stand, and by the time I finally got back across the street to the car I had given up on seeing anything more. But there was one more thing to the beginning of Thursday. It was definitely Thursday by then, almost an hour in.

Thursday for Real

Just as I turned the key in the ignition but before I'd shifted into gear, a pair of headlights hit my rearview, blinding me until I had time to reach up and adjust the mirror. The lights hadn't come from around the corner or from the next intersection back. They came from directly behind me, the parking space behind me, from a just started car. If my eyes weren't lying to me, a black Pontiac, or at least a dark-colored Pontiac. It squealed out of the space, past me, and through the red light at the corner before I had the chance to wipe the phosphenes from my eyes.

I had my suspicions about who might have been behind that wheel. I'll leave *you* to draw your own conclusions—you know as well as I do what kind of car KC drove—as I drew mine.

Okay, I'll tell you one of them.

One of them was that even if the other conclusion I'd drawn was nothing but paranoia, nothing good could come of that first part of Thursday. I needed all six wheat beers to fall asleep at home, and still I slept badly.

Thursday, but Enough Already

I CAN'T DRINK SIX BEERS IN ONE NIGHT. I can't drink six beers in one night and function the next morning. My alarm went off and my brain hurt and my stomach felt like it was full of butter and my mouth tasted like fermented meat if meat ferments, and I realized all of this before I even realized I was awake. I realized I was awake and slammed a ham hand on my clock, shutting off the alarm. It relieved some of the pressure on my brain, but the motion stirred the churn of my guts and I barely made it to the bathroom in time to get the sweet, wheat puke in the bowl. Disgusting, I know, and it still shouldn't be any of your business, but you need to know about my state of mind. My mind was fucking wrecked.

I managed to get showered and dressed, but five minutes of brushing couldn't get the stink off my breath, and I offended myself as I walked to work with my head hung low, sweating booze in spite of the cold. Because I was staring at the ground and focused on only ugly things, I saw that it wasn't rock salt that had crunched beneath my feet the night before—it was the remains of the remains of the guy who'd jumped Tuesday. Mitch. I almost puked again but held it back, breathed deep.

As I got to the front door, it crossed my mind that I hadn't noticed the stray bone fragments and blood smears Wednesday morning. It must have been the Nyquil. Anyway, I know it's hard to clean up a mess that big and there's the danger of soapy water freezing in weather like this, but somebody should really have done something. It wasn't right.

I got to my desk at exactly nine, sat down, and woke up my computer without looking over to see whether KC was there. Then I rested my head against the desk, telling myself I wouldn't do anything but take phone calls all day, that everything else could wait. But as you might have noticed by now, nothing ever works out the way I plan it. As soon as my forehead hit my day planner I sensed someone coming up the hall toward me, sensed someone stopping right in front of me. I assumed it was KC so I didn't even bother looking up.

But I had to look up when I heard her voice, because it was the voice of a her, a woman's voice, a kind of distantly familiar, heard-it-once-before-in-the-long-ago-past-but-definitely-not-everyday-at-work woman's voice.

"You look like you could use some coffee," it said.

My head shot up and the first thing my eyes saw was a huge paper cup of Starbucks held between two feminine hands, almost like they were modeling it. The underside of a pair of enormous breasts—you could tell without even seeing the whole of them—hovered an inch or so above the plastic lid of the cup, and I was about to make my eyes' way up and over them when my eyes and also myself were distracted by a racket that came from the direction of KC's desk. My head shot left against my will.

KC was already on the ground picking up a stack of discs, software or something, scurrying awkward as if to pick up what he'd knocked over as fast as possible, but then slowing his own progress by glancing up to make sure he wasn't missing anything, and also, by the expression of his face, to let me know how pissed off he was with me.

I could tell from that expression that the hands holding the coffee were the hands of April Curtis. I didn't even have to look back, to ask, to know. At that moment I felt like I had won. I wasn't insane and April Curtis wasn't some prank the office was playing on me, and she had brought me a cup of coffee without my having even asked. It didn't occur to me to wonder why.

I couldn't help but flash KC a gloatful smile.

And then, still smiling, I went back to the breasts of April Curtis. I didn't mean to go back to the breasts. Really I wanted to know about the face—the eyes, the mouth, the hair—since big breasts are a dime a dozen. But the breasts were bigger than I'd estimated, even with fair warning, so I tipped back in my chair, and as I did, the rest of April Curtis came into view—chin first, then mouth, nose, eyes, and forehead—and I was taking in the whole person. But the whole person did not look to me like April Curtis, whoever she was. The whole person looked like the whole person of Bonnie Barstow, barely a day different from when I'd seen her last, ten years before.

And how could I have forgotten her when she was the cause of the big thing—the almost witness protection big thing—that I did not want to apologize for on Tuesday which I will now have to apologize for (in the philosophical sense), that is, the reason I had to change my name, and hence didn't get into the Ivy League, and hence never became a philosopher, which is why I am only now getting around to writing my first apology (in the philosophical sense), because I didn't think to apologize in the unphilosophical sense because I didn't have anything to apologize for.

A Monday, Long, Long Ago

THEY DON'T HAVE PHILOSOPHY CLASS IN HIGH SCHOOL. At least they didn't have philosophy class in my high school, so there was nothing for a young philosopher to do but take refuge in the philosophical aspects of senior English. But even that was difficult for me, because my high school was a small one with only two English teachers, and one of them being my father, whose class I couldn't take because he didn't want to give the appearance of favoritism, though actually unfairly high standards would have been more of a worry if you knew him, I took all four years with Mr. Hagen, a dough-faced, red-nosed cretin who didn't do much to compensate me for the fact that there were no philosophy classes in high school.

So, for example, while my father's senior English class was discussing Ernest Hemingway's "Hills Like White Elephants," which I considered an understated masterpiece of proto-existentialism, we were memorizing some Emily Dickinson poem about a snake in the grass. Then we moved on to "Goblin Market" by Christina Rosetti, a stupid fairy tale that we were all supposed to pretend was deep and not actually about goblins. And I only remember it because that was the day Bonnie Barstow came along and ruined everything.

I knew Bonnie Barstow. She'd been in about half of my classes since her family had moved to town when I was in fifth grade. But I didn't know why she'd suddenly shown up in my class that morning halfway through the fall semester. We had the windows open and there was a crisp breeze blowing in, and the sky beyond those windows was overcast but not oppressive, in fact, pretty the way it contrasted with the bright green soccer field and the leaves halfway turned.

Bonnie took a seat directly across from me. Mr. Hagen was one of those teachers who arranged the chairs semicircle, to facilitate seminar-style discussion or to make it easier to look up girls' skirts depending on who you asked, but kept his own much larger desk to complete the circle, so we wouldn't forget who the real authority was.

It seems like I remember the breeze blowing Bonnie's hair around her head even though it probably wasn't strong enough for that.

As soon as she sat down she dropped her copy of the collected stories of Ernest Hemingway on her desk, as though that was what she expected us to be discussing and she wanted to show us that she was prepared.

Fifteen minutes later Mr. Hagen was reading from "Goblin Market" with a lot more passion than usual, like some Lord Byron wannabe, and I got the sense that it was for Bonnie's sake. Maybe because he was facing her and kind of gesticulating right at her. He had to twist his torso to do it because she was sitting to his right and rapt and practically licking it all up. You could see she'd forgotten all about her Hemingway by then. It was making me sick, especially because Mr. Hagen hadn't even bothered to acknowledge to the rest of the class that Bonnie was there, that she was new to us even though we all knew her, much less to explain why.

I expected it had something to do with the tits. Not her presence but Mr. Hagen's undivided attention to them. They were brand new, as big as the ones above my desk Thursday morning, and they'd popped up suddenly, like magic, over the summer. At least it seemed that way, because at the end of junior year she'd been as straight as Ernest Hemingway, and on the first day of senior year she was not. Of course, there were rumors that it wasn't magic, or even biological, but I didn't pay them any attention.

This and maybe more was probably what was going through my mind when I yelled out, "What the fuck is this supposed to mean, anyway?"

Mr. Hagen had just read the lines about "Dewed it with tears, hoped for a root, / Watched for a waxing shoot, / But there came none; / It never saw the sun...." I remember because as soon as he tore himself away from Bonnie and noticed the rest of us were there, then, somehow, guessed it was me who'd spoken up, he repeated the lines back to me:

"Dewed it with tears, hoped for a root,
Watched for a waxing shoot,

But there came none;
It never saw the sun...."

"What the fuck do you *think* it's supposed to mean?" he said.

A few of my classmates gasped or giggled, not used to hearing their teacher cuss. It gave me a few seconds to stall, to try to figure out what it *did* mean to me. The problem was it meant nothing to me because I hadn't been paying attention to the words, because the only thing I'd been paying attention to was the attention Mr. Hagen was paying to Bonnie's tits. So I had to bullshit. Or I thought I would. As I opened my mouth to see what would come out, Mr. Hagen turned back to Bonnie like he needed her in order to breathe, and before I knew it, Bonnie was saying: "Abortion."

"It's not about abortion," I said.

It was not about abortion. People didn't talk about abortion back then, and young girl poets definitely did not write poetry about it, and I didn't need to understand "Goblin Market" or even read it to know that. But apparently that wasn't how Mr. Hagen saw it, at least not when Bonnie was saying the opposite.

"Interesting," he said, in the same voice he'd used while reading us the poem. I was starting to worry I'd have to listen to that voice until I graduated. "Could you elaborate on that for us, Bonnie?"

"Pleasure past or anguish past, / Is it death or is it life?" said Bonnie, or quoted, from somewhere else in the poem. "Abortion. Obvious. Pro Choice or Pro Life. I mean, anti-choice."

I thought, I hoped, she was done, but Mr. Hagen was nodding like a sweaty dog, and it must have been enough encouragement for her, because before anyone else could jump in, she patted the book on her desk and added, "Like 'Hills Like White Elephants.'"

This put me in a tough position, because "Hills Like White Elephants" *was* about abortion, and I knew it without having ever discussed it in my father's class, though I doubted and doubt you could say the same for Bonnie.

Fuck, I wanted to discuss that story with someone, but fuck if I didn't want to discuss it with her. That much was clear already. I wouldn't get a chance just then anyway, because as soon as she'd said it she had the book flipped open to the appropriate place, and then she was reading it in her best imitation of Mr. Hagen's best imitation of a poetic voice, which was, by the way, totally inappropriate for Hemingway.

The whole thing took her fifteen minutes. Mr. Hagen showed no sign of impatience, and did not seem to realize that the story was totally irrelevant to the class, if not inappropriate. Actually he was slavering the entire time. Toward the end I had to bite my tongue to keep from bursting out, and when Bonnie finally finished, clearing her throat and closing her book with another pat, I took my pen and stabbed myself in the thigh, and still I could barely contain my anger.

"Abortion," she said, as though she'd just spelled it in a bee, and Mr. Hagen began to applaud as though she hadn't just spelled it correctly but had won the whole thing.

They both seemed to think the issue was settled, but really it was only just getting started. As soon as the applause died down the discussion started up, the one I always dreaded, the one about the ethics of abortion, with absolutely no reference to anything literary and no interference from Mr. Hagen, who seemed to think he was sitting in some café beside a train station, staring at Bonnie's elephantine hills. Bonnie seemed flattered by the attention, but preferred the opportunity to flex her intellectual muscles.

"You see," she said, "pro-lifers shouldn't be called pro-lifers because that's not the opposite of choice. They should be called anti-choice."

I, philosopher that I was, knew that was a logical fallacy, but I couldn't remember the name of it just then. No matter, the girl beside me upped the intellectual ante before I could even get my brain wracking.

"But abortion is murder," she said.

"It's like the holocaust," said the guy next to her, who was, or was trying to be, her boyfriend.

"That's not what you said when I was late," said the girl to my other side, his ex.

The current or future girlfriend gave the ex a nasty look, and then the boyfriend too, and for a second it looked like things might get interesting, but fortunately for anyone in the room who loved being bored to near tears and completely lacked a sense of irony, Bonnie got things back on track.

"You guys are getting off track," she said. "It's not about personal stuff; it's about rights and politics. It's more of a philosophical issue."

That got my attention, and for once managed to keep it. For a full five or six seconds no one jumped in with a new inanity, maybe because they were all trying, like I was, to figure out what was so philosophical about it. When no one managed anything, I caved in and did it myself, hoping, for the sake of my philosophical vanity, that she didn't have a good answer.

"What's so philosophical about it?" I said.

Bonnie was ready. It had been a setup all along.

"I think therefore I am," she said. "It's like, the mother can think and the baby, the fetus, can't. It's just this blob of skin."

"That *is* philosophical," said Mr. Hagen.

"No it's not," I said, because it wasn't.

But that wasn't good enough for Mr. Hagen. Being right wasn't reason enough to contradict the teacher in front of the obvious object of his affection and affectation. He glared at me and asked to be excused.

"Excuse me?" he said.

I swallowed the urge to tell him he was excused, but worried the gulp looked like hesitation, so I spit out a quick refutation to show it was no such thing.

"It's not philosophy," I said. "She doesn't understand the *cogito*."

"And you do?" said Mr. Hagen.

"I've read Descartes," I said. "It wasn't about abortion."

The latter was true but the former less so. I hadn't read Descartes, I'd only read *about* him. I'd wanted to read him. I'd even gone to the bookstore in town to buy the *Meditations*, but they didn't have it that day, so I got a copy of this book *Irrational Man* that had a longish chapter on him. I hoped it would be enough against such a formidable opponent.

"Well then enlighten us, Mr. Rider," said Mr. Hagen. "What was it about?"

Rider was my name back then, my first last name, part of the reason they called me Knight Rider. The other part was because I didn't drink at the parties in the ravine behind my house. I also didn't attend those parties, because I was never invited, but for some reason, I guess because the ravine was behind my house, I usually ended up being designated driver, hence Knight Rider.

"Descartes wasn't concerned with other people when he made that up," I said. "He doubted everything so much that he couldn't even prove he existed anymore. Then he realized that someone was doubting the existence of Descartes—thinking—and that that person, whoever it was, must exist somehow. *Cogito. Ergo. Sum.*"

I looked at Mr. Hagen. He did not look pleased. I turned to Bonnie. She, oddly, did. Look pleased, that is. She looked like she hoped we could one day have an abortion debate of our own. I hated her. I was a young philosopher, not some blob of skin.

"He's right," said Margo, my main competition for valedictorian. "We learned about it last summer at the Center for Talented Youth."

It was all I needed to go further. I was still looking at Bonnie, and I started to address her.

"By your logic, sure, I could have an abortion," I said, and a couple of the guys laughed, at the idea of me having an abortion I guess. "But by the same logic I could kill a real born baby, too."

There were a few gasps.

"Mr. Rider," said Mr. Hagen.

"Because there's no way I can prove the baby is thinking, that it exists," I said.

"Michael," said Mr. Hagen.

"By that logic I could kill Mr. Hagen, because even if he tried to tell me he existed it could be a trick, like a mirage or an optical illusion," I said, "but the hearing kind."

"Michael Rider," said Mr. Hagen.

It sounded like he really meant it, but I was too close to where I was going, and I didn't want to stop until I was done. I didn't even look at him, just stared right at Bonnie, until the little thrill she was obviously getting from my rant became a chill, and then a look of outright fear.

"I could kill *you*," I said.

I was done.

At that point this was all just an academic exercise because I still believed the world existed, but when I was done with my rant, I was also, it turned out, done with that class, that school, that name, along with my hope for an Ivy League education and along with that the eternal fame and glory of a philosopher. I was kicked out of the room on the spot, suspended by lunch time, and expelled for good the following day, for threatening the life of a fellow student.

One Last Thursday

I DON'T REALLY WANT TO SAY ANY MORE about it right now, and besides, Bonnie's younger sister—she had to be—was standing in front of me. Same breasts, same face, different last name, holding a cup of coffee. I accepted the cup cautiously and with both hands, worried that she might recognize me, though in all those years back home we'd never actually met, and I didn't see any sign of recognition.

"Thanks," I said.

"My pleasure," she said, and she did seem pleased. "I'm April. April Curtis."

She extended a hand and I moved to shake it and almost spilled my coffee because my own hands were wrapped around the cup. It took me longer than you might have expected to set it down safely, and as I did I kept telling myself that my name was Mike Long. My name is Mike Long.

"My name is Mike Rider," I said, finally getting my hand free and out there.

She grabbed it, my hand, reflexively but seemed to catch on something as our hands touched.

"I'm sorry?" she said

Her face became the kind of grimace you want to kiss.

"Mike," I said. "Mike Long. Sometimes I stutter."

I said it to distract her from the slip-up. It isn't true about the stuttering.

"It's true," said KC. "You should see him when he gets worked up about something. His face gets all red and he gets this funny spittle in the corners of his mouth."

That especially isn't true, and April Curtis didn't seem to buy it either, or if she did she didn't like him saying it, because she rolled her eyes at me like there was something between us and it was that we didn't think much of KC, but we didn't dislike him so much that we thought about him at all as long as he wasn't butting in on our conversations.

"Anyway, Mike Long," she said, "I could use a tour of the office, and I hear you're the guy to ask."

I really don't stutter.

"I-I-I heard you already got a t-tour," I said.

KC laughed as though that happened all the time. April Curtis ignored it, ignored him, ignored my stuttering too.

"Yeah, from *Rita*," she said, and the way she said it, it was like she knew a tour from Rita was no tour at all, that it was plain as printer paper that Rita couldn't tell the difference between a post-it note and a paperclip, and I knew then that I'd been wrong about the secret lesbian tryst in the bathroom, and I forgave her for it. I would have given her a tour that very moment and for as long as she wanted, but for the second time Thursday I couldn't stand up, so I checked my desk calendar, and seeing it was blank, as it always was, I pulled my pocket organizer from my drawer and flipped through, hoping she couldn't see its empty pages from where she was standing.

"I'm pretty busy this morning," I said, "but I could probably pencil you in—"

Here I paused and flipped a page for effect, and after I did a little more scanning I tried to seem to find the time.

"How about first thing tomorrow morning?" she said.

I looked up.

"That's exactly what I was going to say!" I said.

"Tomorrow morning, then," she said. "I'll bring the coffee."

She winked, spun on a heel, and walked off down the hall. I noticed as she swayed away that her ass was as nice as everything else, but I kept it to myself because I know the sexual harassment policy front to back, no pun intended, and unlike everyone else I actually followed the rules, too.

"I bet you're feeling pretty good about yourself," KC said, like I wasn't right to be.

But the thing was, I did feel good. It was the best I'd felt all week. My hangover had disappeared, I had something to look forward to, I'd finally seen the new girl in payable, and on top of it all, KC was fuming. I didn't even have to look over at him. It was like I could smell it.

Of course, in the back of my mind I worried that April would somehow learn my secret identity, and there was also the question of how she got the idea to bring me coffee, but my pants still weren't fitting right by the time I finished drinking it.

All in all, it was a good day. Still, later that night, I tossed and turned in my bed until my thoughts turned to April Curtis and my pants started to tighten up again, or would have if I'd been wearing any, and I used a different method to fall asleep. And that is all I will say about that. And that is all I will say about Thursday.

Friday

A LONG TIME AGO, when I first started the job or maybe a couple of months in, someone left one of those one panel cartoons on my desk, from that magazine, *The New Yorker*, I think, that does the one panel cartoons that aren't funny and don't make any sense, but if you can explain to someone how they're supposed to make sense and do a convincing chuckle before or after the explanation—I can't remember which right now—they will promote you and I have seen this happen.

Okay I didn't see it with my own two eyes, but I heard about it. The guy who got promoted was named Richard but they called him the Narrator because legend had it he could explain to you any of those cartoons, even the one with the guy on the golf course, which is the one that got him promoted. But he was so good that right after the promotion someone overheard him explaining the same cartoon in a bar and offered him an even better job on the spot.

I can't explain to you the golf cartoon right now because I never actually saw that either, and it was so sophisticated that no one who *was* there can explain it to me, though they all say he made it perfectly clear and they internalized the lesson of it.

Anyway, someone left one of those on my desk. KC, I'm guessing, or one of the women in accounts who calls every handshake harassment. Or maybe it was just someone who thought I would find it funny. It showed two people, a man and a woman, sitting at a bar. The man was looking at the woman, more precisely the woman's cleavage, which was ample and deep, but you couldn't tell where the woman was looking because the artist, who was probably a pervert, seemed to have forgotten to draw her head.

The caption read: "Male Pattern Blindness."

Stupid, right?

So I whited out the caption, and when it dried I wrote my own caption over it: "Look at that guy with the head." Then I stuck it to the corkboard to see if I would get promoted, but Ms. Miles didn't notice.

I say all that to say this:

It's Friday in the apology, and though I only met her on Thursday, I worry that I may have given the impression that all I saw when I looked at April Curtis, or before that her sister Bonnie, was a pair of big tits. While, as you remember from Thursday, that was literally true of April at first glance, she was much, much more, particularly when you're standing beside her giving her a tour of the office, which is what I did first thing Friday morning. But first, a description of April Curtis, so that you can see that I was paying attention, that I don't have male pattern blindness, and also so that you can imagine what it must have been like, to an extent.

It's true like KC said, and Edward affirmed, that April Curtis was the most beautiful woman to ever work in the office, at least during my tenure, though I doubt KC and Edward ever realized how beautiful she really was. I doubt they ever got past the tits. KC in particular is the type of guy to take pride in his male pattern blindness. And as I said, saying she's the most beautiful really isn't saying much or nearly enough. So let me raise the stakes: April Curtis is one of the most beautiful women I've seen in person. Of course, that's harder to prove by objective standards, so let's just stick to what is demonstrably true.

April Curtis is taller than the average woman, tall enough, like 5'9" or 10", that I feel comfortable describing her as a tall woman. She has long, straight, pale hair, but nobody in the office notices this because she wears it pulled back and up in a very conservative, though not demure—in fact, maybe somehow aggressive, but in a playful way if that makes any sense—bun. Actually, maybe the aggressive comes from the bun but the playful comes from the very slight snaggle to her teeth, which pushes her lips out and up just a little bit, like her mouth is telling her to smile always and it makes you want to smile back. The lips themselves are a little thinner than I usually like, pink, not red, but perfect on her and not at all stingy. Her eyes are brown, and her complexion is very fair and prettiest when she first comes in in the morning, still flush from the cold wind.

So can you see her now as I saw her Friday morning at the beginning of the tour? Or is your male pattern blindness getting in the way? They're big, but not disproportionate, and she covers them up very modestly in dark wool sweaters. It's the posture that makes them so prominent. She has perfect posture. Just try to ignore it like I did while I showed her around.

She was a woman of her word that morning and brought the coffee, which made me very happy, the attention, but it had unexpected negative consequences because the combination of nerves and excitement did not exactly serve to steady my hand. I'll tell you right now I didn't spill during the course of the tour, but only because I kept the cup at my side, clutching it from the top with my right hand, and did not take a single sip the whole time. If I had, even if I didn't spill it all down the front of my shirt, she would surely have seen me shake, which would have made me look ridiculous enough and also like an incompetent office manager who doesn't have the confidence to say what is what and what goes where.

I didn't fuck anything up, but still it wasn't my best tour, and here's the reason why:

As I was showing April Curtis the cabinet where we keep the printer paper and beside it the copy paper, and telling her how the two types of paper had to be kept separate, and how she should under no circumstances load one machine with paper specifically designed for the other, I realized that I didn't actually know the difference between the two types of paper, that I couldn't bring to mind any distinction between them, and that I had no idea what, if anything, would happen if she tried, because I'd never tried it myself. And while I don't think it showed, I worried that she would ask what the consequences would be and I wouldn't be able to tell her, and I'd have to either make something up and look like an absolute idiot, or admit to her that I had no idea what the consequences could be and look like an absolute idiot.

She didn't ask. She took me at my word, and I guess I didn't look like an idiot to her. But I looked like an idiot to myself, and I felt stupid and petty and couldn't imagine how anyone could see me as anything otherwise. I had a sudden impulse to jump out the window like Mitch, the construction worker of Tuesday, but I didn't, and it passed like a wave of nausea.

It came up again as I was showing her the paper cutter, explaining how I kept it sharp with my own personal whetstone and how she should try not to cut her finger off while using it if she ever had occasion to use it. As I said that, I thought to myself how obvious it all sounded and how she must be feeling condescended to, and I wanted to justify my decision to tell her all this with the story of Edward cutting off his own finger. But that was an entirely inappropriate story to tell someone on her first real tour of the office.

The thing was, April Curtis didn't seem to mind at all. She took in everything I said as though it were new to her and succinctly, even fascinatingly presented, like she was learning something at every machine, shelf, and closet, and yet she didn't seem at all stupid or uninformed. It made me hate myself.

I showed her everything the office had to offer, with one exception—my end. I told myself it was because there was nothing there that she needed to know, but the real reason is probably obvious to you at this point: I didn't want to risk a run-in with KC.

It must have been conspicuous, the omission if not the motive, because as I stood in payable trying to wrap things up, I noticed a look of disappointment on her face, the first of the morning, at least that I'd seen.

"It's over already?" she said.

It had been almost two hours, and it's not a big office.

"That's pretty much everything," I said.

"What about your end of the hall?" she said.

"You shouldn't have any reason to go back there," I said, only realizing how callous it might have sounded after the sound was out there. She took it the right way. "I mean," I added, measuring my tone, "It's just me and KC and Ms. Miles, and you know where to find *me*."

"I know where to find you," she said, "but I wanna know what you're up to when you're not giving tours."

By now you probably have your own opinion on how good I am or am not at reading people's tones and signals, but, as little reason as you have, and I had, to believe it, I was sure she was flirting, and so I tried to flirt back.

"Well," I said, gripping my belt buckle, aiming for cowboy but coming off more like Dennis the Menace or Holden Caulfield, "I aim to please."

I blinked hard at how stupid it came out. She must have taken it for a wink because she winked back. I didn't want to press my luck, so I turned and started walking down the hall without looking back. I kind of closed my eyes and wished, as I took my second and third steps, that she'd follow.

She did more than that. She caught up to me and grabbed my right arm with both of hers like I was escorting her into some ball. But not a formal one, because she started sort of skipping along beside me, and I became intensely aware of my right arm—more than aware of, self-conscious about—and I tried to flex it as imperceptibly as I could, hoping the flex would go unnoticed but not the firmness of the muscle, her grip not being very tight. But as I did it, her breast brushed against the same muscle and I yelped a little.

She didn't say anything, but she pressed that breast in further and grabbed my arm more firmly, hard even, and she stopped skipping the better, I think, to maintain position and pace. It felt like there was no way the hallway could last long enough and also like one of those rubber bags my mother used to use for headaches if it was full of warm, soggy Cap'n Crunch instead of ice cubes, which is to say, it felt amazing.

It didn't make any sense. Not the feeling. The feeling was the feeling of actual human contact. What didn't make any sense was that April Curtis was creating the contact, that feeling. It was intimate contact, totally inappropriate for work, with almost no attempt to hide either the intimacy or inappropriateness from me, and it would have been hard to hide from anybody else if there had been anybody else around.

There was no one else around. We were alone in the hallway.

But by the time I noticed it was empty we were almost at the end of it. I got even more worried that KC would see us like that. Because it was such an inappropriate but also intimate thing, and also because it made so little sense, the old theory about this being some kind of office practical joke came back, and I wanted to make sure I didn't get on Candid Camera if I wasn't already.

Finally, as we passed the nook beside the kitchenette where, thankfully, KC was not already eating his lunch, it occurred to me that she might be *hoping* to be seen by KC, that she might be using this inappropriate intimacy to make him jealous, which it would certainly do.

If you ever met KC you know as well as I do that there's no reason to believe that April would ever be attracted to him. But that's just it—it made no sense, and it made no sense that she could do what she was doing to *me*, and so it made perfect sense to worry.

I stopped short of the office, just before the point where we would have come into KC's view if he was there. April Curtis stopped at the same time as me, but she didn't let go and she didn't back off. I looked down at her—not much, because, like I said she was tall for a woman—and she was looking up at me, but not much. It was like the scene of a first and passionate kiss in a movie.

"What?" she said.

There was the chance that she didn't mean anything by any of it, that what was intimate and inappropriate and also amazing to me was just the way she walked down the hall with coworkers. I mean, how do you say to a relative stranger: "The way you are gripping my arm and pressing your breast into it is many things, many good things, but also one bad, which is inappropriate?" I couldn't, because if one of the good things it was not was intimate, at least from her perspective, then how stupid would I look suggesting the rest, and how humiliated would I be on all accounts? My only hope was that KC was taking one of his many cigarette breaks.

I closed my eyes again, took a leap into the absurd, and when I looked the room was empty. But I could sense someone thinking the room was empty, could sense his gratitude at the fact, and realized it was me I was sensing think, and then I felt someone holding on to me and I knew it was April Curtis because I could feel her breast, and no one in the office had breasts that big, no one but Rita. But if it had been Rita that close to me I would have felt a lot more than just her breasts.

I'd somehow dodged a disaster, and, being a cautious man with a philosopher's temperament if not his degrees, I knew, when something of the sort happened, not to press my luck and never did. Instead I pointed to my desk, KC's desk, and Ms. Miles's door, and said, "That's my desk, KC's desk, and Ms. Miles's door," in that order meaning for that to be that.

"Casey?" April Curtis said, loosening her grip a little.

I smiled, because in all the years I'd been calling Kit Carson KC because Kit Carson was a stupid, made-up-sounding name, I'd never once considered that it might sound like I was calling him a stupid *real* name. Casey. Stupid. Like an attempt by parents to create a unique identity for their child out of androgyny and a dash of not very exotic ethnicity. And also because it sounds like the diminutive of case.

"Kay See," I said, "Kit Carson."

"That's cute," she said, like I'd said something cute, though nothing felt cute anymore. "You guys must have a great time back here."

It hurt a little to hear she thought I could enjoy KC's company, because it meant maybe she thought *she* could enjoy KC's company. Unless she was being sarcastic. Her tone was toneless and hard to get a read on.

"Great," I said, not wanting to drag things out only for the sake of the truth, and at that I felt a great slap on my back, and April Curtis must have too, because she pulled away and we spun one-eighty simultaneous without a word between us.

KC's hands were still in the air as we spun, and he didn't flinch when he grazed April, nor when his other hand brushed me. I looked at April and her face was blank, which was disappointing, though not as disappointing as it would have been if it had looked pleased.

"It *is* great," said KC, hands still on our shoulders like a profane pastor. "You should see some of the stuff we get up to back here."

April Curtis stepped back so that KC's hand was just hovering in the air in front of her. Her face was still blank, but KC suddenly looked awkward. I could practically see him weighing his options like his hands were a scale. I got so wrapped up in the visual metaphor that it became real, his hands were a real scale, and I forgot to look at his face to see what decision he made, so I was stunned when his scales suddenly flew up and grabbed my shoulders, and I jumped.

KC laughed, and he was laughing at me, and he wanted me to know it, but at the same time he was trying to make it sound to April Curtis like he was laughing about all the good times he and I had together, or more specifically one, one of the good times, because he started to say one specific one which was supposed to be great but was not, and for a second I thought I would punch him in his face right then and there, like I would not be able to stop myself, which had never happened to me that I can remember, the impulse to actually do it, when he said, "Did I ever tell you about the time we got stuck in the elevator?"

April Curtis's mouth twitched like it wanted to smirk or smile—I couldn't tell which—and she looked over her shoulder suddenly, toward the windows, the skyline, which could not possibly have given her a sign about what was going on in her end of the office because her office was in the opposite direction. When she turned around her face was blank again.

"I've got some work to do," she said, not unpleasantly but not encouraging either.

"You heard it already?" said KC. I clenched my fist. "Did someone up there already tell you?"

April Curtis turned to me, smiled quickly, blanked.

"Thanks for the tour," she said. "I'll see you later."

"Edward?" said KC, working up a lather.

"See you later," she said to KC, barely.

It seemed like KC was about to accuse someone else but caught himself as she slipped past him.

"Later," he said, half turning, to address her back or get a look at her ass. "Happy hour," he said.

She raised her hand and dropped it without looking back, without even breaking stride. What a beautiful stride it was—a little bit of swagger and a hint of strut, but still office-appropriate.

"Happy hour?" I said.

"Yeah," he said.

I was supposed to follow up, to pry the details out of him, but I didn't bother, and here's why—he'd taken the first pretext to try to tell the elevator story, which meant that he would take the next that night, would *make* the pretext if he had to. I was assuming the happy hour was that night because that night was Friday and what kind of idiot organizes an office happy hour for Saturday or Sunday? Strike that.

KC turned out to be exactly that kind of idiot, but anyway I assumed it was that night, and I assumed he would tell the elevator story, and so I had no intention of being there, because I assumed that once the story got out—to April Curtis, that is; it was already out to everyone else—she'd never flirt with me again if she even looked at me.

That she'd flirted with me in the first place was why I was so sure that she hadn't heard it already, even though everybody knew it and loved to repeat it and tried to be the first to tell any new hires. There were people who hadn't even worked there when it happened who told the story as though they'd been in the elevator *with* us that day, when obviously they hadn't. It was just me and KC. But that didn't stop them all from ridiculing me and creating a toxic and hostile work environment.

For a second I felt like Mitch again, the construction worker from Tuesday whose bone shards and maybe other parts I'd walked through on the way in that morning and also before that, but I didn't feel like pitying myself, and I don't want you to pity me. It had been a good morning. My first in a long time. I decided to go to lunch and remember it, to try to recreate the feeling of April Curtis's breast against my arm and keep it fresh, because I assumed, given all of the assumptions of the previous few minutes, that I would never be feeling it again.

At lunch I played through the whole morning on fast forward and got stuck on the end, the part where April Curtis looked over her shoulder and out the window and somehow knew that she was needed down the hall. Of course it's exactly the kind of line you use when you're trying to get out of talking to someone you really don't want to talk to, a bore, or a cretin, or a creep, and how I hoped that was true. But she'd seemed so guileless during the course of the tour. And anyway, why then, at precisely the moment KC was going to tell the elevator story?

I spent the rest of the afternoon standing in the spot April Curtis had stood, looking over my shoulder for a sign of anything that could have given her a sign of anything, work-related or not. All I saw were the tops of buildings and the middles of buildings and the clouds. I eventually decided that there was no sign, but it was nice standing where she'd stood and doing what she'd done. I was sure that soon enough she'd lose respect for me like everyone else if they'd ever had it, and I wanted to memorialize the time before she became like everyone else, to commit it, not just to memory but to my body.

KC tried to distract me, by mentioning how much fun *tonight* was going to be—happy hour, I guessed—and by asking me what I was doing, but I tuned him out as well as I could.

I looked over my shoulder. I faced forward down the hall. I looked over my shoulder.

When I faced forward for the last time, April Curtis was walking my way. I glanced at the clock and it finally occurred to me that *that* was what had tipped her off. Maybe she'd seen it and realized she'd wasted the whole morning with me, hopefully not in the bad sense of waste. By then it was five to five.

I sat down, hoping it would look to her like I'd just gotten up to stretch for a minute and not almost four hours. She stopped in front of me and rested a hand on my desk.

She tried to lean on that hand casually but it didn't really work because she was so tall, and she stood upright, taking her hand with her. It was kind of funny and she knew it was kind of funny even if she hadn't meant it to be in the first place, and she laughed first and I laughed with her. And don't think for a second that KC hadn't been watching the whole thing, and don't think he didn't laugh two or three times as loud as the both of us put together, because he did, probably because he didn't actually see the humor in the situation. We stopped laughing and April Curtis looked dismissively at KC then back to me.

"So what are you doing tonight?" she said.

Firstly, she said it to me, and second, here is how I could tell she had said it to me: she said it like a parody of someone asking someone else what someone else was doing tonight, and someone else got it and understood that no response but maybe a little smile was called for at the moment, which he—I—did, smile, and KC did not.

"Happy hour?" he said. "Happy hour, right?"

"You going to happy hour?" said April Curtis.

That question begged a direct response, and at that moment the direct response was: no. Actually that had been the direct response about five minutes before, and now it was more like: what are *you* doing? Do you want me to go with you? And if I do will you devote your whole attention to me so that neither KC nor anyone else has any chance to tell you the elevator story? And if, somehow, someone manages to get past our defenses and tell you the story, will you put an arm around me and remind me that you like me?

Which, yes, I know is not actually a direct answer, which is why I gave an indirect answer, but much shorter, and much, much less revealing.

"I don't know," I said. "You?"

KC was already putting on his ball cap and he paused to wait for the answer, which also turned out not to be direct.

"I don't know," she said. "Where is it?"

"Educated guess?" I said with a glance KC's way. "Applebee's."

April Curtis cracked up. KC finished putting on his cap. He obviously didn't see what was so funny but he had to say something.

"Applebee's my ass," he said. "That's some bullshit eating good in the neighborhood shit. We're going to—" He paused here, whether for effect or because he had to think of a new place to go to happy hour I'll leave up to you to decide. "Chili's," he said, "and get some of those big onions." He picked up his briefcase and came over to me. "And you're coming, Knight Rider."

He hustled off down the hall, probably torn between trying to convince April Curtis to come too, and having to tell everyone else we weren't going to Applebee's after all, but Chili's, because he wanted his baby back or something.

I didn't have time to think any more about it because he'd given me something else to think about, which was the Knight Rider comment, which, as you know, I didn't want him saying, and which, as you also know, meant something much different to April Curtis, if it meant anything to her, than it meant to KC.

April Curtis made a face like it meant something to her, a kind of concerned biting of the bottom lip which, while worrisome, was also very pretty.

"Knight Rider?" she said. "Why'd he call you that?"

You can see why it was not the time to tell her the truth, right? But also, since it is my policy to tell the truth, I didn't want to lie. So I told *a* truth. I said, "I don't know," which is somewhat true, because I don't know why he still insists on calling me that when I've asked him not to and told him I don't like it. Except I do. Not like it, know. I do know why he calls me that, and it's because I've told him I don't like it, and as a threat. But it's true that I don't know why, because I don't know why at the deepest levels of the human condition there is a basic drive to do to people things they don't like.

Anyway, April Curtis seemed to accept it, shook it off.

"So are you coming?" she said.

And I said yes because I half wanted to, but I more than half didn't want to leave her to think about why KC had called me Knight Rider, and even though there was a chance, hell, it was practically a given, that KC would do it again at happy hour, and probably worse, would almost certainly tell the elevator story, the stakes were higher now, and I wanted some control over the situation, or at least an idea of what was happening, if complete control wasn't possible.

But a minute later it didn't seem so impossible, because of a sudden change in the immediate situation, and because of a sudden idea the sudden change gave me.

The sudden change in the immediate situation was this: that as we made our way down the hall we realized that the office was completely empty, that everyone had either gone ahead to Chili's to be welcome there, which is the corporate slogan as it turns out, or had gone on home because they didn't want to be welcome or happy that hour.

There was that and there was also the fact that April Curtis maintained an appropriate, but not unfriendly, distance from me as we walked down the hall, as though she sensed that appropriateness was more appropriate to the situation.

Those two things combined gave me the idea of how to take control of the situation, which was to tell the elevator story, the real one, which is slightly less humiliating than KC's version, thereby preempting KC, who tended to work certain details to his advantage.

So when we got to the elevator bank, I looked around one last time to make sure that we were really alone, and then I pressed the down button and told her I had a story to tell her and please not to say anything until I was done.

The story I told her was this, more or less, because this, and not KC's version, was how it happened:

ONE MORNING, a few months into my career as office manager, I was running late for work, because I'd had serious trouble falling asleep the night before—I hadn't yet begun the experimenting with sleep aids I've mentioned already and so had slept through my alarm—and also because I decided to stop at the bodega for coffee with the hope of making my head less cloudy. Even so I was only a little late, i.e., I got in at what passes for punctual with KC.

KC and I got on the elevator at the same time, and I'm sure we said hello to each other and probably had some sort of conversation, but I honestly don't remember because I was so tired, which is why I kept guzzling my coffee. When the elevator stopped, neither of us thought much of it. The elevators in the building are notoriously bad, which I've mentioned. So we pressed the alarm button as we always had before with the expectation that we'd be moving again shortly as always before.

In the meantime I guess we probably did some awkward talking and I kept drinking my coffee, and you're probably getting a sense by now if you didn't have one already of where this is going. The meantime turned into a long time and before I knew it the coffee got empty and I had to pee.

Soon all KC would talk about—and I remember this explicitly—was how long it was taking and how badly *he* had to pee, and that made me have to pee worse, and the alarm was really starting to get on my nerves.

Eventually I put my cup down thinking I could always use that if I absolutely had to, but KC snatched it up right way. He took it to the corner opposite me and faced the walls and before I knew what he was doing I heard the stream of his piss hit the cup. The sound of his pissing made me have to piss worse, and the end of his pissing made him have to piss less, and when he placed the cup, sans lid, back on the floor and turned around, I could see his relief and it made me angry.

The little box we were in started to stink almost immediately. Add to this the fact that KC had more on his mind with less on his bladder and sat down on the floor with his back against the wall and tried to turn everything into one of those movies where everybody just sits around talking, the *Breakfast Club* or *Pulp Fiction*, and I felt like I was about to burst from everywhere.

And then I did.

I pissed myself while screaming at KC for having taken the cup without asking. And don't think he wasn't terrified of me at that moment. He was. He didn't say a word back to me, and it wasn't until months later that it turned into the story of an idiot getting scared and pissing himself when the elevator got stuck for fifteen minutes or fifteen seconds depending who you asked, rather than the three hours of truth, which conveniently left out the details of the coffee and the coffee cup and KC's terror of me, and the fact that one of my outbursts might have been a secret trigger to the elevator because that's how soon the elevator started moving again afterward.

And that was the elevator story as it actually happened, and when I got to that point I stopped and waited for April Curtis's reaction. Her first reaction was one of waiting for me to continue. I watched as it went from one of waiting to one of realizing I was done.

"You're done?" she said.

I prepared to slink away forever, never to meet her eyes again much less to feel her breasts against my arm.

"That's it," I said.

I looked away.

"Because you told me not to say anything until you were done," she said.

"I'm done," I said.

"I already heard that one," she said. "Or one a lot like it. Unless there was another totally separate time when you flipped out and pissed yourself when the elevator stopped for, like, fifteen seconds?"

"KC told you?" I said.

"Rita," she said, "my first morning."

"Even Rita," I said.

"Also Edward," she said. "I knew it had to be more than fifteen seconds."

"Yeah," I said, because how else was I supposed to respond?

I don't know how long we'd been standing there—it was my first time telling the story out loud—but I only noticed it had been a while when I heard the bell and saw the green arrow pointing down.

"You were trapped in there three hours," she said, as though what I'd done had made perfect sense. "It's not like you still wet the bed or anything."

The door opened and she held it open with one hand and gestured for me to enter with the other.

"Yeah," I said, and went in, all the way to one of the back corners.

She followed, pressing the button for the lobby. The doors closed. She stood facing me with her back to them, and though things had gone as well as I could realistically have hoped, I clenched and prepared for the kiss off. The elevator started to descend.

"You don't wet the bed?" she said.

"N-no," I said.

"You don't stutter either?" she said.

I froze. I really don't stutter, and she must have known it was true because she laughed, and not like she'd gotten me, either, but more like she got me, if that makes any sense. I felt understood, which if you know my philosophy, you know that's a pretty big deal to me.

She went over to the other back corner and kind of slouched, resting a shoulder blade against each wall, gripping her skirt at the thighs, and letting her eyes close like she was exhausted.

I, thinking I'd dodged another disaster, did what I do when I dodge a disaster and moved onto something else. In this case the only thing to do was watch the numbers descend in their LED panel, so I watched, but around the fourth floor I started to hear something coming from April Curtis's corner, some kind of tap tap tap.

I figured she was probably drumming a finger against the wall, but when I looked over, her hands were where I'd left them, clenching the skirt. Then I thought feet, so I looked down, but her feet were still and the tapping continued. Then it stopped and so did the elevator. April Curtis opened her eyes, looked my way, and gave me a sleepy smile that was so pretty.

The door opened and she stepped toward it, and it was only then that I saw the little puddle, just the tiniest damp patch she'd dribbled on the floor in solidarity with me. I heard the door try to close and fail, and looked up and she was there, holding it open again, still smiling, wide awake now, even mischievous.

"I know it'll be dry by Monday," she said, "but it's still funny to think of KC stepping in it."

Stepping in her pee didn't sound like such a bad thing to me, and I doubted it would to KC, either, but I knew what she meant, and it was a funny gesture, and it made me happy, and it was sexy to think how she must not be wearing underwear. But that wasn't the best part. It wasn't the part that made me happiest. The part that made me happiest was that she called Kit Carson KC. I'd been calling him

KC for six years and it had never caught on with anyone else. To tell the truth, as stupid a name as Kit Carson is, I worried that it might sound cool to some people, that it might sound cool to her. But she'd called him KC, and there was no way she could think that was cool.

Chili's is only a few blocks away from the office, and we walked there in silence, and she kept a distance from me, or we kept a distance from each other, but somehow the distance and the silence were more intimate than any number of breasts against an arm.

Happy Hour

I KNOW THAT HAPPY HOUR ISN'T A DAY. Still I'm setting it apart for ease of reference. As you might have noticed, there was plenty to apologize for during business hours Friday.

I'm not apologizing for happy hour, not even in the sense of justification. What I did might not be legal—it depends on whether *stalk* is a fighting word—but I didn't think even KC would be bitch enough to try to press charges, not after Sunday. Regardless, I don't regret it.

Happy hour is only here to connect Friday with Saturday.

The sign on Chili's said "Welcome to Chili's," and while I'm pretty sure it says that on every Chili's sign, I felt welcome at first, probably because I walked in with April Curtis. April Curtis felt welcome because the minute we walked in, all eyes turned to her, all conversations stopped, and everyone took the time to greet her. Then, grudgingly, me.

At least it seemed like everyone, because everyone from the office had come, everyone except Rita and Ms. Miles, and they were all sitting and standing in the bar area just inside the doors.

We returned everyone's greeting, and KC, still wearing that stupid ballcap, shoved deeper into the booth, half-crushing poor Edward between himself and the wall, and patted the space beside him. It was more than enough space for one, and nowhere near enough for two. I imagined it still ass-warm and shivered a little. I looked at April Curtis and saw she hadn't noticed or was trying to seem like she hadn't.

Somebody, Cindy I think, said, "We need more chairs," and everybody kind of sat there looking awkward like chairs were at a premium in that Chili's, everyone but KC, who only wanted one more addition to the party. I still didn't feel unwelcome.

"Here's room for one," he said, still patting the space beside him, a little desperately now, like the pigeon in that experiment, "right here."

"There's plenty of room for both of us," said April.

She shoved me toward the bench. I resisted at first, then decided it had probably been enough time for KC's warmth to escape a little.

Those vinyl seats have a low specific heat. I made my way to the bench, slid in, and stopped before I made contact with KC. I was right about the seat but wrong about the weather in general. I could feel the heat pulsing off of KC—a combination of his natural temperature, a couple of beers already, and anger. I made it a point not to look at him.

April Curtis slipped in after me. She managed to get a little more than a thigh onto the edge, then, rather than push me in further, she wrapped a calf around mine, hooking it at the ankle. It was inconspicuous, and I don't think anyone noticed, but everyone definitely noticed when she raised an arm and rested it on my benchback. It was on the back of my seat and not touching my shoulder at all, so it was familiar but not necessarily inappropriate, but still everyone at the table was awkward again and I felt KC's temperature rise, caught a faint whiff of cat piss from his armpit even though it was locked hard between his arm and torso.

I made an even bigger point of not looking at him, though in that position it would have been impossible to look at him without contorting my torso or neck. I focused on the feel of April Curtis, which was warm but not sweaty and smelled like fabric softener with a little bit of body.

"So what are we drinking?" she said.

"Two more glasses!" said KC.

I couldn't tell at first if he'd given the order to anyone in particular because the place was pretty crowded with people wanting to feel welcome and it was hard to tell the staff from the clientele what with all the polo shirts, even in that weather, and also because KC accompanied the order with a grandiose gesture of the arm between him and Edward, meant, I guess, to emphasize the order itself and to prove his authority to order at all. I saw a mousy blond woman in a black button-up roll her eyes and switch directions and knew his wish was her command.

He saw it too, and then gestured toward the pitchers at the table to show his openness and generosity, but there was nothing April or I could do with them short of drinking from the pitchers themselves, which we were not about to do. We all sat there, uncomfortable, silent, as though the glasses were the keys that would unlock the doors against which our various abilities to, and desires for, fellowship pressed and banged from the other side, and as flowery as it might sound when I put it flowery like that, it was pretty much true, because pretty much only booze could relieve the stress of our proximity to each other, even if our proximity to each other was a choice in that case.

This was proven by the way the silence broke shortly after the glasses were served up. The conversation gained momentum slow but steady as the pitchers lost their bubbles and then their contents, and were refilled, emptied, and refilled again, until finally we were all joking and laughing like we were actually enjoying each other's company, and we were, even if the company smelled on one side increasingly more like hot wool than fabric softener and on the other ever stronger of piss, and our collective cacophony could have put a family of apes to shame as we shrieked with maybe overstated laughter mostly at the expense of Ms. Miles, because she was the only one besides Rita (and who would make fun of Rita out loud?) who was not there, but also because she was the authority, there in spirit to be mocked, and never, for once, at the expense of me, until first one, and then another, all the way to maybe half of them declined another round, citing family obligation or simply the need to get home as cause, and the noise began to die, maybe a little less slowly than it had begun, but yet not as completely.

As things quieted down my sense of dread grew, because even if I'd felt for the most part like things were going well, my sense that KC was still just waiting to pounce never quite left me, and the loss of our kinetic energy seemed to increase his potential, and it seemed that as the noise died down, so did his heat, as though it were withdrawing to his core, preparing for one final, intense burst.

And then there was another uncomfortable pause, and I stopped breathing and waited for what he would give me. But he didn't give me anything. He didn't get the chance, because April Curtis beat him to it, gave *him* something.

"Did I ever tell you about the time I pissed myself in the elevator?" she said.

Remember, I'd been holding my breath, and when she said that, it all escaped violently. I suppose I looked like I was drunk. This was not helped by the way April Curtis was laughing, just as hard, if more naturally, beside me. She looked like she was drunk, too, and she was, and *I* was, and I liked it for once. I tried to calm down, to catch my breath, to keep from passing out.

"I pissed myself in the elevator too!" I said.

April's reply came out haltingly and hackingly, but still comprehensible, at least to me.

"But I was only in there fifteen seconds!" she said.

Everybody froze who wasn't frozen already. Then a couple decided to follow through on those family obligations without even trying to cover for the fact that it was our outburst that had them going so soon. The rest decided, you could tell by looking at them, that they'd leave at the first opportune moment, except KC, who it turned out, was intrigued rather than angry. We'd forgotten to anticipate the potential appeal, at least to some men, of the opportunity to picture April pissing as she described it.

"Wait," said KC, "when did this happen?"

April and I had pretty much calmed down by then, enough at least that I picked up on the sound of her sneering.

"Jesus, Kit," said a voice from the other side of KC. Edward was the only one on the other side of KC, but I didn't recognize the voice as his. It sounded so confident, and also pissed off. "It didn't happen. Obviously she already heard the story about Mike," and here he faltered a little, finally sounding recognizably Edward, because only Edward, besides April and I, knew that he was one of the wheres she'd heard it.

"I don't get it," said KC.

"She's clowning you," said Edward. "She's clowning us all."

"Except for me," I said, and here April Curtis's arm did finally slip to my shoulder as if to say except for him, though I'm pretty sure everyone was either gone or too gone by then to notice.

KC had outpaced us all with the drinking, but for some reason, I guess because he has so much experience, it was only just catching up to him; you could see it descend on his head like a helmet made of fog.

"No," he said, trying to shake it off but only making it heavier.

"I'm going," said Edward.

Edward stood up straight, but had apparently forgotten the table was there in front of him. Soon it wasn't. Soon it was tipping forward, away from him, from KC, me, and April. Fong and Cindy, who were the last ones left on the other side, caught it and righted it before it flipped all the way, but not before the dregs of what beers remained remained no longer in their glasses and their pitchers, and a few of those glasses and a pitcher had crashed to the floor, bouncing rather than shattering, being only plastic.

Edward had spilled again. He didn't make a big thing of it this time, but it was spectacle enough already. The glasses and pitchers that had stayed on the table were still rattling when Edward slid it forward to give himself the room to get out without having to get past us. He slipped away, and Cindy and Fong followed, and then there were three, all scrunched together facing the same direction.

As the slow-eyed server came over to clean up our mess, I tried to take stock of the situation. Obviously April's joke had had a bigger effect than we'd expected or intended, or even, in my case, at least, hoped for, but just what the effect was was hard to say. Was it a ding-dong-the-witch-is-dead-type of situation or just the quickest way to clear a table and a room?

"I don't get it," said KC.

The waitress had picked up the last of the plastic glasses and was wiping down the table. A Mexican guy was pushing an industrial mop bucket in our direction. I was waiting for someone to tell us to leave, but no one would. That's one thing about the places KC likes to go—they're so anonymous that people don't even notice you're drunk. If you want proof, look how long it took us to get more beer.

"Another pitcher," said KC.

Obviously I didn't want another pitcher, but the waitress was off, no time for me to cancel or call her back.

A lot of things went through my head just then, among them a mild disappointment at having this dragged out any longer, and also a little thrill at the prospect of dragging it out longer. The former is obvious; the latter resulted from the realization that April and I were going to get the opportunity to explain things to KC point by point, in great detail, and he would listen, even appreciate, our making fun of him to his face, at least until he realized we were making fun of him to his face.

That is, if April Curtis stuck around. It looked for a second like she was going to take off like the rest of them. As she slid away from me, shook her arm out, let it drop to her side, and stood up, I felt a disappointment way more profound than the one I'd felt when KC had announced his inclination to stay by ordering. I worried I'd been fooling myself. But my worries were for nothing. She walked around the table, pulled out the chair across from me, and sat down with a look that told me we were in this together, and if that hadn't been enough to allay my fears, the way she rested her foot on top of mine, comfortably but not too flirtatiously, was.

The waitress placed a pitcher and three clean pint glasses in front of us, and I felt welcome all over again, the last few minutes having served to sober me up some. I poured because KC had other things on his mind.

"Okay," he said, slurred if that's possible in only one word, "explain this to me."

April Curtis took the lead.

"You know how you seem to think it's funny that Mike peed himself in the elevator?" she said.

I knew she was with me, but it still hurt to hear it put like that.

"Not just me," he said. "Everybody."

"Everybody," said April, "including me. Just in a different way. So when he and I were in the elevator on the way here, I decided to try it myself."

She was leaving out some of the psychological intricacies. I figured it was out of modesty, so I jumped in once I was done pouring.

"See, you're an asshole," I said, "and you were trying to use the elevator story to embarrass me, but she wouldn't give you the chance."

It sounded kind of unlikely as I said it, but April Curtis's foot stayed right where it was, and her expression said we had an understanding.

KC, on the other hand, did not have an understanding of anything. He didn't seem to have noticed my calling him an asshole, but he didn't seem to have absorbed much of the rest either, and so we spent a long time telling and retelling and explaining the story. The more we all drank, the more KC sobered up, and I watched the realization trickle over him, like water in a shower, that he'd been owned, but also saw him trying to suppress his growing fury, probably to save face in front of April Curtis. Still his face was getting hot red and the scent of cat piss practically hovered above the table.

I was only getting drunker, and I knew it. My sense of dread grew. I tried to make myself small, to take little sips at long intervals to keep both drunk and dread from getting worse if better wasn't going to happen.

It was KC who finally changed the subject.

"So does anybody have any big plans for the weekend?" he said.

It was amazing how lucid he suddenly sounded after all that beer, not a single syllable slurred. I, on the other hand, knew that I'd better not drag out my answer.

"Nothing," I said, because I almost never had any weekend plans, though I was hoping something might come up that weekend, and hoped my answer might help make that happen.

What I was not hoping was that April Curtis's sister would be coming to visit.

"My sister's coming to visit," said April.

I was taking a longish sip of beer as she said it, and of course it went down the wrong hole and started me coughing, though fortunately I didn't spit anything out, and I managed to get my glass safely to the table in the midst of my fit.

KC took the opportunity to pound me on my back, which believe me, it hurt, and still aches at certain angles as of this writing, and it also did nothing to help the coughing die down, but the coughing did die down eventually, and KC continued pounding for a minute after that.

"You need some more beer to clear you out," he said.

The pitcher was empty. My glass was empty. I'd only taken that last longish sip to make it empty, because I was weary and wary and ready to go.

"No," I said, but it came out in a scraping groan that ironicized the rest of the sentence. "I'm good."

"You're what?" said KC.

I cleared my throat.

"I'm ready to go," I said.

"Me too," said April. "Do you want to walk me home?"

I did. And I didn't. Did for obvious reasons. Didn't for obvious reasons if you can think back far enough. Recall, I had a history with her sister if her sister was Bonnie Barstow, and she had to be. It was more than a resemblance; it was a match. I had a sordid history with the sister who was coming to visit, and while I didn't have any reason to suspect that she'd invite me along—which I'd have to turn down—I worried that she'd want to talk about her sister, since her sister must have been on her mind, and that in my drunken state I'd let something slip, some indication that I was not a complete stranger to Bonnie. Unless she was talking about some other sister. Remember, I didn't remember Bonnie having a sister in the first place.

But still, I couldn't let Bonnie's sister walk home alone, in the city, at night, and I wasn't going to shove her in a cab when she lived so close to me.

"I'll walk you," said KC.

April's foot pressed down hard on mine. It had been there the whole time, but the pressure had been so gentle that I'd forgotten it. The increase meant I was supposed to do something, I could tell that even in my drunken haze.

"Not you," I said. "You're getting in a cab headed for the Main Line. I'll get April home."

As I signaled the waitress for the check, I could feel KC smoldering beside me. The catpiss scent was probably still there too, but I guess I'd been immersed in it so long I wasn't registering it anymore.

"Take her home?" said KC. "*Whose* home?"

"We live in the same neighborhood," April said.

The check came, papercutting the tension. KC put down his card and said it was on him, and the way he said it, there was no point in arguing, nothing to do but thank him. But then we had to wait for the waitress to run it, because it's wrong to run out on the guy who's footing the whole bill. I think this might have been why he did it, that it might have given him a hundred fifty or some such dollars' worth of satisfaction to make us sit there with him in awkward silence for another few minutes while we waited.

And the silence was awkward.

Finally the waitress brought back the card and the receipt, and KC made a big production of tipping extravagantly and signing with a flourish, and as he flipped the vinyl-bound receipt-book closed and set the pen down beside it, he turned to April Curtis.

"Did I ever tell you about the time our boy Knight Rider here stalked the new girl in the office?" he said, in that weird pirate voice he'd used the time we'd gone to watch the game.

Maybe by some really strict and hazy definition of stalking I had stalked the new girl in the office. But the fact was, she liked me better than she liked KC, and that had nothing to do with any of the things that I'd done that some extremely anal and legalistic type might call stalking. Why she liked me better, I could not explain and still can't. She just did. And also I'd asked him, KC, I'd *told* him not to call me Knight Rider, and I'd had enough.

"Let's go outside," I said.

I meant it like in a movie, like I am going to fight you now, whether you like it or not, and in the movies when this happens, the man who says it, because it's always a man, gets up and makes for the door without looking back, expecting the man he's called out—that's always a man too—to have some honor and follow him out and not to attack him from behind but to wait until they're both outside and ready for the mano a mano, all of which was appropriate considering Chili's is supposed to have a southwestern theme. So that's what I did, except with a little more staggering than in the movies because I'd had a lot to drink and hadn't stood up in a few hours.

But as I got to the door I worried that I'd made a mistake, because I didn't want to fight, and I'd never fought before, and KC had, though he hadn't looked very good at it back when I'd been attending his classes, and also because I'd just assumed KC had a sense of honor. For all I knew he was still sitting back there in the booth telling April Curtis how I'd so-called stalked her, and in the meantime probably making me sound about ten times more maniacal than I really am. So I was torn between hoping he didn't have a sense of honor and hoping he did.

In any case, there was no turning back, figuratively or literally. I pushed open the door and stepped out into the night.

Saturday

That might seem like a contrived and cliffhangerish place to leave happy hour, but the truth is, this is not a movie, and happy hour, which actually lasts two, at least at *that* Chili's, had been over for five, and I just didn't feel like barging in on the situation to go back to Friday night when Friday night has no more relevance to you than happy hour. But I know for certain that Saturday began about the time I walked out that door, for reasons I will explain later and also for reasons I will explain much later.

So Saturday began.

But first I need to tell you something. Remember that caveat before happy hour? The one about how I'm not apologizing for those actions? Well if you don't, go back and read it now.

Now that you remember the caveat from happy hour I can tell you it goes for Saturday too. And Sunday as well. This is the last time I will tell you that I'm only telling you this in the interest of truth, philosophical truth. *Caveat* is a Latin word, philosophical, lends this a gravitas. *Gravitas* also is a Latin word.

Saturday began with gravitas. It was warm out, unseasonably warm. Or not unseasonably warm but warmer than it had been all week. The damp air interacted with the cold, dry surface of the city to create something more dense than a fog but less than a mist.

I don't know why, but the first thing I thought when I stepped out into it was maybe it was warm enough that they could finish cleaning up Mitch. You know, spray down the sidewalk with a hose or something. This after registering the warmth. I admit it was a strange thought to have spontaneously given all that was going on, but it's the truth, and anyway I didn't get to think about it any harder just then because of all I had going on.

I heard the door open behind me and I spun around.

KC stood silhouetted in the entranceway, the dim light around his edges violent enough in the dark night, refracting off the mist—I'm thinking of it as a mist now—looking solid, bulwarkian, and sober, though looking sober is easy enough when you're standing still. That last bit in reference to KC and not the mist or the light.

KC stumbled forward, not unsoberly but shovededly, by April Curtis, who now stood silhouetted in the entranceway, looking fucking lovely.

I lost my concentration for a moment for obvious reasons and when I got it back KC was lunging toward me.

It's the truth that I thought he was lunging toward me, *at* me even, though now I admit it's possible he was just stumbling forward shovededly again. But as I said, I'd lost my concentration, and I was feeling antsy, and also I'd called him out only a minute before, which for some reason is seeming like an eternity just now.

Long story short, I slugged him and he went down.

I remember the thud of his body as it hit the ground and the pain in my right fist as it dropped back to its side, and, somehow, more pain as it opened, as though my fingers wanted to be a fist forever and never a hand again. It was the first time I ever hit a man, and though it didn't feel bad, even the pain didn't feel bad for the moment—not good but not bad—I hoped it would be my last. I was never going to hit a man again.

I didn't have to. KC got up pretty quickly but obviously groggy and staggered backward facing me. It was as though I had transferred my intoxication to him, and for the first time I thought about the meaning of the term punch drunk and decided the meaning was that. I felt a kind of clarity I associate with an autumn Saturday afternoon, when the air is crisp and so is my mind because I didn't have to take anything to get to sleep the night before because I didn't have to get up early for work, and I decide to sit on a bench in the park and read some Hegel and feel every sensation with all of my senses. That kind of clarity, if you've felt it.

I thought to myself that if it was still that warm on Saturday I would go to the park and feel things. I didn't know it was already Saturday. It would be a little while before I would realize it was Saturday.

So thinking it was still Friday, but otherwise clear and lucid, I watched KC stagger back and then stop, a little hunched over with a hand over an eye, and finally straighten up, hand still on eye.

"What'd you do *that* for?" he said.

"You had it coming," I said.

He rubbed the eye and then let the hand fall to its side. The eye was reddish and a little swollen, but that was all.

"Fair enough," he said, and I agreed.

"Let me grab you a cab," I said.

He took a step backward.

"It's okay," he said.

I looked around to see if there were any cabs nearby that I could hail for KC, and noticed April Curtis was standing in the shadows, her expression hard to read. It made me a little nervous. She'd seen the whole thing but hadn't said a word. Suddenly the most important thing to me was knowing her feelings on this situation that made me feel neither good nor bad but clear. It was way more important than trying to find KC a cab, and anyway the street was empty.

"You'll take a cab?" I said.

"I'm okay," he said.

"No," I said. "Take a cab. Don't drive."

"I'll take a cab," he said.

I was ready to leave it at that, because, as I've said, April Curtis was the most important thing, and also, if I'm being one hundred percent honest, which is what I'm trying to be, maybe I was hoping that he wouldn't take a cab, that he would drive home and, not, you know, die or kill a little kid or anything—though what would a little kid be doing out that late?—but maybe crash into a utility pole and maim himself pretty bad. In a sense, he still owed me a DUI.

As I was maybe feeling the hint of that thought somewhere toward the back of my skull, but so far back it was practically not in my head but behind me, really, April Curtis ran off suddenly, and for a second I was ready to drive *myself* into a utility pole. Instead I watched April Curtis running down the street as if she hadn't had a thing to drink all night—that fast and effortless—and assumed that was it between us.

She hit the corner and stopped on a dime, waving a hand in the air. The minute her hand hit the sky about five cabs appeared out of nowhere and screeched to a stop in a line in front of her, each, I guess, hoping to be the one to take her home. Seeing how KC was just behind her, I figured one of them at least would be willing to take his fare as consolation prize, so I didn't need to stick around. I turned the opposite way and headed for home.

The streets were empty, eerie, and the mist and the loneliness reminded of a French New Wave film, *Rumble Fish*. Even in the light from the streetlamps things seemed colorless.

As I walked I started to get the feeling there was someone behind me, close behind me, like a couple of body lengths. I picked up speed. I shoved my hands deep in my pockets and made fists of them. The pain in the right reminded me that I never wanted to punch anyone again, and also to use my left if I had to. Whoever was behind me matched my acceleration.

My first thought, which is always my first thought in a situation like that, was that someone had emerged from the shadows of an alley, probably a beggar or a mugger. But whoever was behind me didn't have the requisite shuffle of a beggar and was dragging things out for a mugger.

The only thing I could come up with was that maybe KC hadn't ended up in one of those cabs after all, that he'd been more conscious, even humiliated, than he'd seemed, and that with April Curtis out of the way, he was ready for revenge. I kept walking a second, listening for the sound of steps behind me, and they were there, maybe a little closer, but they refused to become anything more—the steps of a particular person, drunk or sober, friend or foe.

I let my right fingers go hand and clenched the left ones tighter to remind myself that those were the ones to use, but by then my hackles were up, or whatever it is that happens when something is about to happen, and I was ready for anything, but mostly to be done with what was going on. I stopped hard and spun, hoping to catch KC off guard.

But I didn't. I didn't even catch April Curtis off guard.

"You gonna hit *me* too?" she said.

It hurt me to think she could take me for the kind of man who would hit a woman. I wondered if my hitting a man in front of her, arguably unprovoked, the day after I'd met her, had contributed to that impression. For someone, me, who'd made it twenty-eight years without hitting anyone at all, that would have been unfair. So it took me a while to understand she was joking even after she cracked up and bent over with a belly laugh.

I didn't know what to do, so I just stood there and watched and thought how pretty she was, even in such a ridiculous position. She let the laugh end at a perfectly natural point and stood up still sighing some, with a look that was a little more big sister than I was comfortable with, especially given I knew I was older. But she still looked so pretty.

"You don't fight much, do you," she said.

"Was it bad?" I said.

"No," she said, with a look that was not at all patronizing and that said that what I'd done was not at all bad, either in intent or execution, that she maybe even kind of liked it. "Just like you don't do it often or for no reason."

I smiled and probably flushed, because that was as good as I could have hoped for, probably better than I should have.

"Walk me home?" she said.

I spun back the way I'd been going and offered my arm as gallantly as I could. She accepted. We walked.

I realized that, without thinking, I'd started walking us toward her place. I didn't want to give her the impression that I knew where she lived, because I didn't want to have to explain why. So I started asking questions, since I had plenty of them anyway.

"Where do you live?" I said.

"This way," she said.

Apparently she didn't feel the need to elaborate.

"Why didn't you take one of those cabs?" I said.

"Because I'm walking home with you," she said.

We walked awhile in silence.

I wanted to ask her why she'd hailed them in the first place, then, but I also didn't. I guess I was supposed to though, because after a block or so, she said, "It was for KC. He may be an asshole, but I didn't want him to drive home."

"You didn't want him to hit a utility pole and maim himself?" I said, hoping she actually did, like me.

"I don't care so much about him," she said. "I just don't want him running over some kid."

It was what I wanted to hear, but it also rang a little hollow.

"At this time of night?" I said.

I pulled out my phone and checked. Half past midnight. That was when I realized that the fight had probably happened on Saturday.

"It's the city. There could be kids out this time of night," she said. "But yeah, I guess I don't want him to get maimed."

I was a little disappointed, but I consoled myself that at least she was a better person than me. And I was walking her home. Or she was walking me.

It was hard to say until we got to Pine, which was the turnoff, for both of our places but in opposite directions. To get to my place, right; hers, left. By then I'd forgotten to remember not to let on that I knew where she lived, because of the conversation and because I was concerned with who was walking whom. I wanted to be walking her, to keep her safe, though I sensed she didn't need it, like she hadn't needed me to fight for her honor, which I knew was not what had happened but hoped was what it looked like even so.

I turned left on autopilot and she grabbed my arm again, this time with both of hers. We were walking slower than before, and closer, and I could feel her breasts against me at each step. It was quiet for a while except for the occasional passing cab.

"So how'd you know where I lived?" she said.

I made a point to keep walking. I wasn't ready to come clean. That was when I remembered that she'd told KC at happy hour that we lived in the same neighborhood.

"How'd you know where *I* lived?" I said.

"I don't," she said.

"But KC," I said.

"What about him?" she said, genuinely confused.

"At happy hour you told him we lived in the same neighborhood," I said.

It took her longer to respond than it should have.

She finally said: "I was just saying that 'cause I didn't want him walking with us."

It was plausible enough and also flattering. I decided not to push any further, because I felt like it would be pressing my luck.

Quiet again, a warm quiet. She drew closer and I imagined we looked like a real couple, a couple that had just had their first little disagreement, and the guy had won, which is why I was walking so tall and flexing my arm again to be strong and silent for her.

But I hadn't won, and in fact I was losing insofar as I didn't even realize the spat was still going on, and it was *my* fault because I hadn't answered the question that started it, only deflected it with another. But like I said, I was just thinking about how good I felt and how we might look, so when we stopped in front of her building and she turned toward me, I was thinking maybe I would get a good night kiss, and that's about it.

"You never answered my question," she said. "How'd you know where I live?"

The truth slipped out.

"I staked out your place the other night," I said.

April's eyes went wide but she didn't seem angry or scared.

"Staked out?" she said.

"Because I didn't believe you existed," I said. "I kept missing you in the office, and then someone left your HR file on my desk, so I sat out here on the stoop to see if I could see anything, but I didn't."

I pointed to the stoop across the street. She grinned.

"You didn't see the fat lady?" she said.

"I saw the fat lady undressing," I said, "but not you."

"That's because my windows face the back alley," she said like a plain and simple fact.

"I'll keep it in mind," I said, also like a plain and simple fact.

She smiled.

"I wasn't going to kiss you tonight," she said, "but now I am."

She moved in with her mouth open and her arms up. Our lips met, and then our teeth and our tongues and our chests and our hips and our knees. It was warm and boozy and sticky-dry and also beautiful, and my hand hurt and my pants tightened and April pressed closer until we were done, and then she pulled back and looked at me, arms still around my neck.

"I'm not inviting you up tonight," she said.

"Okay," I said, relieved. Seriously.

"If you'd figured it out about the back alley I would have invited you up tonight," she said, laughing.

"Okay," I said, not really taking her seriously.

"Do you want to have dinner with me and my sister tomorrow night?" she said.

She meant tonight, Saturday, and I didn't want to, and I started to wonder why she had to go and ruin everything by bringing up her sister before I realized she didn't realize that she threatened to ruin anything by doing that.

"No," I said.

"Okay," she said, not like it was okay but not like she was disappointed either, and she gave me a peck on the cheek. "Night."

"Goodnight," I said.

I watched her climb the stoop and, remembering how she'd peed in the elevator, tried to see if I could see up her skirt, but the skirt was too long and the stoop not steep enough and it was all so nice anyway. She slipped her key in the lock and turned as she turned it.

"There's an entrance to the alley right around the corner," she said.

She opened the door and went in without waiting for my reply, which is okay because I didn't have one. I watched the door as it closed after her and stood staring at it for a while. I figured I was supposed to go stand in the alley and watch for something, but I didn't because that's creepy. I turned and headed home, slowly.

I should have been happy, despite the whole sister conundrum. We'd put the elevator story to bed, possibly forever; I'd won my first fistfight with a single punch; and a woman, a beautiful woman, whom I'd maybe behaved a little inappropriately toward, had kissed me despite or because of it, and it looked like we might have a future. But really I was just exhausted and also sad.

I didn't have any trouble falling asleep. Maybe you're surprised.

I WOKE UP LATE IN THE MORNING just as easily as I'd fallen asleep, feeling surprisingly fresh and a little melancholy. My right hand hurt, but the weather, as far as I could tell from the windows, mirrored my mood—deep blue sky with lots of billowy clouds and leaves blowing down the street like an advertisement for cool breeze. My first thought when I saw it was my promise to myself from the night before that I would go to the park and read if the weather was exactly like that, so I took a long slow shower to get really clean, the kind of clean you can't get during the week when you've got to get to work on time, threw on some jeans and a sweater, tossed some Hegel in a bag and headed out.

There's a park a couple blocks west of my place, very fancy, the park of choice for most people, but I don't go there because it's the park of choice for most people, and though I like people-watching as much as the next guy, I guess I like reading *more* than the next guy. You know what I mean by that but take it how you want.

Anyway, my decision to go east to the park that's almost as nice but never as crowded had nothing to do with its proximity to April Curtis's place, and this is how you will know I am telling the truth: Remember, April Curtis's sister, who I assumed was Bonnie Barstow, was visiting, and I had no desire to see them, or at least her. Bonnie. Besides, I *always* went to that park to read, long before April Curtis, and though I couldn't have known this at the time, the next part of the apology will provide plenty of evidence of that, evidence provided and corroborated by people other than myself, i.e. April and Bonnie.

So I got to the park and I reached into my bag, and here I will have to admit to you that I have actually been lying to you this whole fucking time and I'm sorry, but it was a small lie and I really didn't think it would come to anything. But it has and so here I will apologize for once not in the philosophical sense: I'm sorry.

Now let me apologize in the philosophical sense: It was not Hegel in my bag. I don't read Hegel. Nobody else does either, which is why all of the Hegelians these days call themselves Marxists, Darwinists,

Secular Humanists, or Beatles fans. That is why I also didn't write an honors thesis on Hegel and Knight Rider. I mean, who the fuck can get with the idea that everything's getting better all the time?

Everybody, I guess. Everybody but me. But I'm right, because I've been paying attention to the way things are really going.

I wrote my thesis on Descartes, and the reason why I left that fact out was because Descartes is always getting me into trouble. He got me into trouble in high school like you remember, and then again in college, this time along with Wittgenstein.

You've already seen my summary of Descartes, and while it's kind of young, it's fundamentally sound and I stand by it. Here is a quick thumbnail of Wittgenstein: words are important but they have no inherent meaning. They're just a model of things themselves that people made up so that they could try to understand each other.

I'm not as confident in that summary as I am in the Descartes because I never actually read Wittgenstein. I mean, who could make it through that crap? And anyway, if words have no inherent meaning, I got enough from Wikipedia to back up my basic idea which was that Descartes couldn't have been a very good doubter because he forgot to doubt words, which is weird because that's what he was writing in and also what supposedly got him out of his mess.

If Wittgenstein had been there to tell him, "Renee, that is a girly name, but that's okay, because language is just a system of models that somebody made up and that includes names. What is not okay is that you think "think" is more than just a model for what you think you're doing. You think it is the actual thing you're doing, and it is not, so please doubt *think* also, and every other word, and see if you can still prove you exist. Hint: You cannot," all of this in Latin, by the way, or French, then what would have happened?

I will tell you: the world would have ceased to exist right then and there. And I know this because that's exactly what happened for me the minute I realized it. The world just ceased to exist for me.

This is actually a much better thing than it might sound like to a non-philosopher. For example, I realized immediately that I wouldn't have to read that Wittgenstein, and the fact that I didn't pass my thesis defense was of no consequence, because there was no thesis defense, or it was at least a matter of radical doubt. So the fact that I did or didn't graduate with honors as I did or didn't indicate on my résumé, even though I actually did or didn't graduate from college, did or didn't finally matter, and I'm glad we finally cleared that up.

But the best reason to doubt the existence of everything by finally doubting language was that there was no reason to believe my father was a pervert. That was not something I lied to you about, just something I was trying to leave out, because the story is so clichéd it sounds like a thirty-minute sitcom that morphs into an hour-long after school special. But now that I see that the events of Saturday are forcing me to bring it back in, if only in its most barebones form, here goes:

I MENTIONED I WAS KNOWN AS Knight Rider because of my name and because I was always designated driver. Well, make that always minus one.

Parents go out of town and I seize the opportunity to host instead. Party rages. I get pass-out drunk. Parents somehow contrive to return home suddenly and break it up. Everyone manages to get away mostly unrecognized but for Bonnie Barstow, who is almost as drunk as me. Father drives her home. Next week she's in *my* English class instead of *his*. Only the two of them know what actually happened, but rumors are flying all over school—everything from a pathetic proposition to outright assault. The severity of my punishment for my outburst in class comes from suspicion on the part of the authorities that my father put me up to it.

For the record, he didn't, even in a world that exists.

Here's the thing: I wasn't exactly a part of the grapevine. You have to believe me when I tell you that I had no idea what Bonnie Barstow was doing in my class that day, that I'd spent the entire weekend grounded, recovering from a brutal hangover, and barred from contact with the outside world, not that the outside world was much interested in contact with me, and that my outburst was strictly literary. I only found it all out after my father and I had moved out of town and changed our names.

So the world's nonexistence was a huge relief, almost as huge as when I finally got undeniable proof that my father was not an actual pervert. That undeniable proof came Saturday afternoon, at the park.

I WAS SITTING THERE READING THE *MEDITATIONS*, really absorbed and enjoying the crisp air on my face, when I heard a woman's voice say, "*That's* the guy you're stalking?"

My head shot up and my eyes saw two April Curtises walking toward me. I shook my head and it was two Bonnie Barstows. Another shake and it was one of each. Any of the preceding perfectly plausible in a world that doesn't necessarily exist. What seemed implausible was that they were both smiling as they walked toward me.

"You don't look a day older than the last time I saw you," one of them said.

I assumed it was Bonnie, considering the statement would have been ridiculous coming from April.

It was uncanny how much alike they looked and sounded.

"You know this guy?" said the other one, April.

"Know him?" said Bonnie. "I got him kicked out of school!"

What is probably already perfectly clear to you took me a minute to sort out, but by the time April followed up I had an idea where we all were. It still seemed more like a soap opera than a Saturday at the park.

"*That's* Knight Rider?" said April.

"It's Mike Long, now," I said.

"Yeah," said April, "I've always known him as Mike Long."

The way she said it, it sounded like she'd known me more than two days. Not like she was just trying to *sound* to her sister like we had history. She said it like we actually *had* history.

"Well back in high school he was Mike *Rider*," said Bonnie. "That's why we called him Knight Rider. That and because he was always designated driver."

She seemed to realize something as she said it, and before either April or I could jump in, she added, "Oh my God, how's your Dad?" more like he'd been involved in a minor fender bender the week before than like she'd played a major part in ruining his life, if it existed.

"He's fine," I said.

My father *was* fine, by the way, at least for a while. After he failed as an English teacher, he took some courses in accounting and realized that his way with words was not actually a way with words but a way with numbers. So in a way, I guess, she hadn't ruined his life.

"Tell him I'm sorry about the whole getting him fired and making him change his identity thing," she said.

She hadn't explicitly admitted she'd made it up, but suddenly, and for the first time since college, the whole world was real to me. What's more, the idea that the world could possibly not exist seemed incredibly stupid. I'd felt a beautiful body against mine the night before and tasted its beery mouth, and the question now was not whether those things were part of a person of their own, a beautiful and strange and maybe-a-little-off person, but why Descartes, why anyone, why *I* would ever want to consider the possibility that was so obviously not a possibility that she was just some hallucination or the machinations of an evil god. I mean, fuck Descartes. Even his book suddenly felt like a dead thing in my hands, and I decided I wished only one thing didn't exist and it was that book. But I wanted answers about everything else. I wanted my father to exist, pervert or not.

"Are you saying he didn't do it?" I said.

"Do what?" said Bonnie.

"Whatever you said he did?" I said.

"I never actually said he *did* anything," said Bonnie. "I just told my parents he was weird when he drove me home. I didn't want to get in trouble for being drunk, and they didn't want to have to deal with me, so they ran with it."

"Was he weird when he drove you home?" I said.

"Everybody was weird all the time," she said. "Him. Mr. Hagen. Every boy in school. I hated them all for letting me get away with everything because of my tits. Except for you. I hated you for not letting me get away with *anything*."

I should have hated *her* at the moment. I mean I think I had the right. But I'd been hating her for so long when I didn't think I had the right that I just didn't feel like it anymore. Besides, she had something like a point, and though her reactions were a lot more than equal and opposite to the actions she described, they, and the way she related them, seemed real, an affirmation of the world's existence. I decided to let her get away with something.

"Fair enough," I said. "I mean, not really, but."

But she wasn't looking for my approval and was already on to the next thing.

"Still reading Descartes?" she said, and I think I detected a trace of condescension in the way she said it.

"No," I said.

I tossed the book behind me, my right hand reminding me that it ached in the real world.

It was dramatic, but the moment called for something dramatic, because whether I wanted the book to exist or not, the book existed, and now it existed in grass that existed, and would until someone else who existed came along and picked it up, or until the rain and snow pummeled it until it existed as something else, like the pulp it had been before they put the words on it.

"I read Descartes in school," said April, "in French. I majored in French."

"I know," I said.

"How?" she said.

"I read your résumé," I said, "that's how I found out your address, remember?"

"You two are perfect for each other," said Bonnie.

She laughed, and April laughed, and I felt a little left out, which was further proof of my existence.

"How?" I said.

"You're a Peeping Tom and she goes to the park every Saturday to see if you're here," said Bonnie.

I didn't like being characterized as a Peeping Tom, especially because I'd only ever done it once and done it wrong, and because that sounded a lot worse than going to the park every week, but I overlooked it because I wanted the dish on the going to the park every week thing.

"Peeping Tom sounds worse than just going to the park," I said.

"Not if you follow the guy home from the park and then follow him to work and then spend a year trying to get a job in his office instead of just sitting down on the bench next to him and starting up a conversation," said Bonnie.

April shoved her. It was somewhere between playfulness, animal aggression, and sisterly hatred.

"It was supposed to be a seduction," she said. "You just ruined my endgame."

"I just added some self-consciousness to it," said Bonnie. "Kierkegaard already did what you were trying to do. Letting the seducee in on the endgame makes it more interesting." She turned to me. "See, I can do philosophy, too. I'm a professor of it."

"I'm an office manager," I said, but I was thinking I would not be for long.

"I know," said Bonnie. "April keeps me up to date. No accounting for taste."

"It wasn't taste," said April. "It was random at first."

"Now it's not?" said Bonnie.

"I thought you were a philosopher," said April. "A thing can only be random once."

"So now you want to marry him," said Bonnie, "ergo, no accounting for taste. No offense, Knight Rider. You're cute enough."

If her intent was to inject self-consciousness into the seduction, mission accomplished. But what did they really think of me?

"So are you going to dinner with us?" said April.

"I don't think so," I said.

"Okay, then, I'll see you tomorrow," said April.

April bent down and gave me a kiss on the cheek, and then left, leaving me with a lot of questions, first among them being how April could know she would see me tomorrow—that is, Sunday—when we hadn't made any plans and I didn't have any plans she could know about. The thing about a world that exists—you can have a lot of questions and all possible answers seem pretty random until they happen, at which point they start to have been kind of inevitable.

Take April's "random" comment, for example. What had she meant by it? That she'd just "randomly" picked a guy in the park and it happened to be me? Or was she using it more colloquially, as in I was just walking through the park, saw a guy I was attracted to, and I "randomly" decided to follow him home? Because everything exists, there are all these thoughts running through my head, but also running through hers, so what seems random to me and maybe also to her is not actually random but the combined existences of us interacting, which is beautiful even if the outcome is bad, and I'm not just saying that because I already know the outcome of this particular interaction, or at least part of it.

So I decided to head home and just think all night, about the seduction and what could happen after the seduction, about what I would be when I was no longer office manager, which I decided would be soon because it did not seem an appropriate career ambition in a world that existed, about thinking, and how we can share and understand the thoughts that happen between us, and ask a lot of questions, and not worry about the answers, which is the beginning of philosophy.

When I got home, the place was a mess and there were seventeen messages on my machine. Yes, I still have a landline and an answering machine, and I know that sounds pathetic, but there's a perfectly logical explanation for it: it's for my father. I live with my father. I was trying to keep that out of my apology because living with your father is not very philosophical. Also because I was trying to have a little bit of love story in there, too, like in Kierkegaard, and sharing a one-bedroom walk-up with your father is not exactly romantic, even though he crashes mostly on the couch.

It was true what I said, that when we went into hiding, my father discovered that his way with words was actually a way with numbers, and he *was* fine for a while. Then he threw out his back lifting a banker's box without bending his knees only to discover that his way with pharmaceutical opioids was even stronger than his way with numbers. The disability checks were enough to keep him comfortably numb but not sheltered so I moved him into my dorm room, which, fortunately, was a single, then dragged him along with me when I got the job here. He needed the landline because his limbs were too limp to operate a smartphone, and I wanted to be able to get in touch with him in case of emergency. I never had any emergencies, though, and he only used it to call the guys he met up with at the all-night diner to trade pills.

But what if there *had* been an emergency? Seventeen calls at four rings per! How could he know it wasn't me, dialing and redialing while being hacked to pieces by a rival mob of geriatric pharmajunkies who would have accepted a mere amber bottle of oxycontin for ransom, while he lay there nodding on the couch, filling my living room with his sour old man smell? Nothing can get me as mad as my dad.

I tried to calm myself like usual by thinking about all he'd been through: forced to leave home, wife, and job—everything but me—at a moment's notice, and still willing to, no, insisting on bringing me along, though his need to leave was half my fault, albeit unintentional. But thinking about that only made things worse, because after talking to Bonnie that very afternoon, I knew the whole story was false, that my father had been lying to me the whole time.

I hadn't been at fault, half or otherwise; he hadn't been at fault; there hadn't been a fault at all! And yet my father had driven us out of town like a pair of outlaws, Butch and Sundance, or that other one, Oedipus and Antigone, and in the process, he'd erased me, ending my chance of going to an elite school and becoming the philosopher everyone expected me to be!

If ChlorAmmo had existed at that very moment, I would have cleaned up our whole mess on impulse, without so much as a thought, and this apology wouldn't just be impossible; it would be unnecessary. But ChlorAmmo didn't exist yet, and wouldn't for a few more hours, so I did the only thing I could think of to vent, which was to deliver the standard litany to my semi-conscious dad about how he'd ruined my life.

"**Harvard, Dad.** Or at least Vassar. I could have gone to Vassar," I seethed.

He turned his head slowly from side to side, unsurprised but aware that I, or at least someone, was in the room.

"Do you know what kind of doors Vassar can open for a young philosopher?" I said.

He opened his eyes. It took them a long time to focus, longer to find me, and when they did, they didn't show any sign of recognition, much less concern.

"Do you?" I said, raising the volume, and when he didn't answer, I brought the hammer down: "Neither do I, because I never went to Vassar!"

I could tell I'd been recognized, but the sheer effort it took had me losing steam. I tried to keep it going: "Or Amherst! Or Bates! Or Bowdoin! Or ..." I stumbled, mumbled "at least Bucknell."

I was capable of going on longer. I had memorized the *USNEWS and World Report* rankings every year since I'd graduated high school and could recite them in numerical or alphabetical order. Obviously this time I had chosen alphabetical. But my father had heard all that before, was used to it by now, already preparing to dismiss me. What he didn't know was that I had new evidence, an eyewitness account, a personal confession, and I had to get to it before he went back to watching unproduced movies on his eyelids.

"I saw her today," I said.

His eyes flashed suddenly. I could tell he was fully present, and that, somehow, he knew who I meant. He glazed over on purpose, but I had him.

"Who?" he said.

"Don't play dumb," I said.

He closed his eyes, and at first I thought he'd managed to nod off again, but when he brought his sagging arm up to his clammy forehead I could tell he was thinking.

He finally spoke: "Son, I dreamed of permanent revolution, but what I got was perpetual war. It wasn't my choice to make."

Ever since the doctors got him hooked he's sounded more like an oracle than a philosopher, but I could usually get some sense out of him.

"She said nothing happened," I said. "She said you didn't do anything."

He replied more quickly than I expected.

"She told you the facts, Son, but not the truth. I did not lay a hand on her, nor did I say a word. I did not even look much her way, just a glance in the mirror every now and then. She was draped across the backseat, intoxicated and vulnerable. Her vulnerability did not appeal to me, Son. For me the strong-willed girl of slightly-above-average intelligence, stone sober if a little rundown and irritable at the tail-end of a long school day, seeking out ways to argue the intersection of classic literature and current affairs. Hemingway and abortion. Eliot and sexwork. James Joyce and coprophilia. That was the version of her that filled my mind as I drove her drunken husk home. In my head, she was the initiator, and the things she initiated were glorious but unspeakable, and so I will speak no more of them, Son, except to say that at the height of our imaginary passion, I looked into the mirror to refresh my memory of the actual thing, and met her eyes, or rather her eyes' reflection. She was staring at me as aggressively as she had in my fantasies, but her gaze did not express desire, Son; it expressed awareness, as though my own eyes were projecting the scene in my brain out onto the mirror where she could see it in reverse. She knew, Son, not vaguely, but in high definition detail. She knew the placement of every limb, every appendage, the velocity and viscosity of each drop of sweat and fluid on our bodies in my mind's eye. And she knew that I knew that she knew, because that look of awareness slipped briefly into horror before ossifying into disgust, a look of disgust she maintained defiantly until the very moment we pulled up in front of her parents' house, Son. That look told me she would scorch my earth if she could, and I was impressed, aroused, and devastated."

"She did say you were a little weird on the drive home," I said.

"That's just the thing, Son," he said. "It wasn't weird; it was perfectly normal. It was the way of things. If anything, her acknowledgment of it was weird. That was the innovation, a tactic only, Son, indicating a new strategy, a nuclear option: that of not allowing me, or any man, I'd guess, to imagine those things in her presence, or to delight in the belief that she knew and could do nothing about it. The only thing, soldier, was to retreat. But our retreat was not tactical. It was strategic. Endless retreat. I have consulted with the joint chiefs of staff and we are in complete agreement."

It was ironic, him using this extended military metaphor, considering he'd dodged the Vietnam draft by wearing lace panties to his exam, pubic hair trimmed into the shape of a heart. He'd admitted it when I came back to my dorm room on September 11, 2001. He told me those methods wouldn't work anymore and he was going to have to shoot me in the foot, was all ready to head over to Walmart and buy a gun. I managed to convince him to wait until I was at least called up. Now here he was talking like he was the commander in chief himself, the old men at the diner his trusted war cabinet.

"Isn't that kind of a grandiose way to talk about the battle of the sexes?" I said.

"Is that what you think, son? The battle of the sexes? What I'm talking about is the war on terror! And I *am* terror, Son. Which I suppose makes you terror's son."

It was the oracle of the temple of Apollo at Delphi that declared Socrates the wisest man alive. But here's the thing about oracles: they were just old ladies in caves getting high off of ethylene fumes that rose up from a crack in the ground and rambling. There was no reason to listen to them, just like there was no reason to listen to my father.

NOW FOR A DIFFERENT TYPE OF RAMBLING. All seventeen messages were from KC. As I listened it became clear quickly that KC had no memory at all of what had happened the night before and that he was turning to me for any help I could offer in recreating the evening's events. So after listening, I called him back, because one great thing about existing is that you can try to convince people that what actually happened was not what happened.

"Knight Rider?" he said after only half a ring.

"Mike," I said.

"Sorry. Mike," he said.

"What's up?" I said.

"What happened?" he said.

"What happened when?" I said.

"You too, huh?" he said.

"I guess," I said.

"April too," he said, which threw me. "Listen," he said, "she can't make it tonight, but tomorrow we're going back to Chili's and try to figure it out."

"Who?" I said.

"Me, April, and you," he said. "The ones that were there."

Obviously I had no desire to go back to Chili's, welcome or not, but if April had already agreed I had to go. I trusted her, in a way, but I didn't want her alone with him, and I also needed my chance to skew the story. I told him I'd meet them at seven and hung up.

I didn't spend the rest of Saturday thinking; I spent it in action.

I remembered my time in KC's Mixed Martial Arts class, not the fighting he'd done, but the fact that he'd done it. It was possible he'd gotten better. I was used to the usual pranks and tricks, but what had happened at happy hour was big. I was worried I might be in real danger.

Then I remembered what had led, indirectly, to my time in KC's Mixed Martial Arts class. My big business idea. ChlorAmmo. I didn't want to get into chemical warfare, but I figured I could use it as a deterrent if I needed to.

I headed to the back patio with some window cleaner, chlorine bleach, a roll of duct tape, an old surgical mask from the SARS days, the goggles from a snorkel set I bought when I was thinking about going on one of those singles cruises but never used because I never went, and a pair of pink rubber gloves, the kind you get for washing dishes or gardening.

It would have been cooler if there was thunder and lightning out there, mad scientific, but it was actually a pretty nice evening. A cool breeze made the electric lines sway a few inches over my head, but there was nothing you would call wind.

I put everything down on the concrete of the patio and looked around to make sure none of the neighbors were watching. They weren't. There wasn't a single light on, which was weird because it wasn't that late.

I put on the mask, gloves, and goggles. I squatted down, peeled back a corner of the tape, and, wrapping the two bottles completely from bottom to top, brought ChlorAmmo into existence.

I pointed the nozzles at a thin strip of ivy climbing up the back wall of the yard, and squeezed the dual triggers. Nothing happened. I figured maybe plants were immune, and anyway, I only needed it as a deterrent. I gathered up my things and went inside.

Back in my kitchen, I took a Sharpie and wrote "ChlorAmmo" on each side of the duct-taped bottles. I didn't have time to figure out a good logo, so I just used block letters. Then I placed it on my kitchen counter and looked at it from several angles, satisfied with each.

I thought: Socrates had his hemlock, and I have my ChlorAmmo. I am a different kind of philosopher. For Socrates, philosophy was made of dialogue; for me, it's action. For Socrates, it was something the world did to you; for me, it's something you do to the world.

I put the bottle in my bag so I wouldn't forget it.

I never got around to cleaning up the mess in my place, and I don't think I need to tell you I had a tough time falling asleep.

Sunday

Not to beat a horse dead, which is not a cliché but could be construed as a Nietzsche reference, I think I know why Descartes decided to doubt the world. He said it was because it sometimes seemed like his senses were playing tricks on him and he wanted to find out if it was really his senses or if it was actually God. The thing is, why would anybody get suspicious just because their senses played tricks on them? It's like that drawing everybody's art teacher did for them in junior high that's either two faces in profile or a candlestick, to blow everybody's mind. It's pretty cool when you're twelve, but probably doesn't change many lives, and anyway, it's not a trick of God but of every junior high art teacher. I refuse to believe that the great genius of the seventeenth century thought like a twenty-first century seventh grader, so I can't help but think it wasn't the tricks themselves that scared Renee. I think he just didn't like surprises. Same with that other one, Philip Roth. Anyway, part of the reason that I'm glad the world exists again is that I like surprises, and I like them to be surprises. Don't get me wrong, I'm not against finding the reasons behind things. I know how fucking magnets work; you know I use elevators; and I dislike infant mortality as much as anybody else. But when it comes down to it, I don't care if Sisyphus is happy pushing his rock up a hill or not. I just think he's an idiot if he's ever shocked when it rolls back down. And as you can see from my life, if I didn't like surprises, I would have drunk the hemlock a long time ago without even bothering to apologize.

That is a fucking lot of philosophical references in only one paragraph, even if it is a long one.

Anyway, here is proof of the theory I just told you: sometimes even *I* don't want to be surprised, and the best way to not be surprised is to stay inside like a philosopher.

Sunday was one of those times, so I stayed in and had all these ideas and got intertextual about things. Which is a way of saying I didn't leave the house to do my reading on Sunday, and also masturbated (left handed because my right still hurt) frequently and furiously, and between the two reached a state of something like equanimity. What I did not do was clean the place, so it only got messier. Blame it on my hand.

If this all sounds gratuitous, consider what I was about to have on my plate again. That's right, Chili's. And, in a less literal way, KC and April, and, while I couldn't have known it at the time, Bonnie Barstow.

I GOT TO CHILI'S EXACTLY ON TIME. My equanimity got a little shaky along the way, but it shattered when I opened the door to see the three of them sitting at our table, laughing, with full and half-full glasses in front of them and two empty beer pitchers on the tabletop.

I almost turned around right there, but I didn't, and that's how you can tell I'm a different kind of philosopher, because it was a complete surprise, and I didn't doubt for a second it was real. My eyes weren't playing tricks on me.

I walked toward them, hoping for another surprise. I was hoping that the laughter of at least one of them was joyless, or meant something other than what it looked like, because it looked like April Curtis was enjoying KC's company.

KC must have sensed my approach because he was the first to turn my way, and as he did, I saw the bright black shiner on his left eye and winced. I had done that to him.

"Knight Rider!" he said, pointing to his eye. "You did this to me?"

Just then April and Bonnie looked over and they both stopped laughing and stared at me like I'd knocked out their own boyfriends unprovoked. I searched their glares for a sign that this was some kind of joke, that they hadn't already given me up, but their faces were blank at best. Things were not looking good for my hope. I figured there was nothing for me to do but acknowledge it.

"Yeah," I said.

"Asshole," said April, and she turned away.

I started to get these twitches at the corners of my mouth, and I probably looked like some cartoon character about to cry, but really the feeling was much more complex, so complex that I still don't know what to call it. Whatever it was it was at the extreme end or ends of the emotional spectrum—not anger but rage, not sadness but despair, not confusion but mania. Maybe those extremes form a circle that pulls you to a tense equilibrium, because I felt like I couldn't move, or I couldn't will myself to move. I felt the ChlorAmmo throbbing in my bag against my back, but this wasn't an appropriate time to use it, and I didn't have the strength to reach in and get it anyway. My lips kept twitching against my wishes, but eventually they stopped too. Eventually.

"I wouldn't have guessed you had it in you," said KC.

Bonnie had turned away when April had.

"I saw it in him from the first time I met him," she said.

April didn't respond in words, but she nodded affirmation, and that was when things started to seem even more suspicious, because she'd said on Friday night that I didn't seem like the type who fought much. Now I know that there's not necessarily a contradiction between not seeming like the type to fight and wearing the potential like a costume, but still, it's a really fine distinction, maybe finer than you'd expect in a Chili's. It seemed much more likely that she'd either changed her mind or was fucking with me.

But if she was fucking with me she was doing a really good job, and so was Bonnie until she spoke up again.

"Who invited *him* anyway?" she said.

It was completely over the top, even if she didn't know the answer. But she did, because that was how April had known on Saturday that we'd see each other on Sunday. The real question was who had invited *her* (obviously it's a rhetorical question; April invited her), because if we were there to recreate the events of Friday night, what could she add? The other real question was how could KC be so oblivious he couldn't see right through it? That's also rhetorical, basically.

"I invited him," said KC. "Besides, I probably deserved it. I mean, he's asked me like a billion times not to call him Knight Rider."

Things just kept getting weirder. If I hadn't decided just the day before that the world existed, I would have been certain at exactly that moment that it wasn't April fucking with me but God the evil genius. Instead I decided it was possible because it was happening. What wasn't happening was anybody inviting me to sit down. I told myself to sit down anyway, because it was about time and because my body seemed to be working again.

The only available seat was between Bonnie and the wall, where KC had been sitting Friday night when I called him out. We were doing a very bad job of recreating the events. I stepped closer and hovered over Bonnie a minute, but she didn't take the hint.

"Can you scoot over or let me in?" I said.

She shook her head, not as in no, but as in I had a lot of fucking nerve. She moved over anyway, and I moved in to find myself sitting across from April Curtis, who wouldn't even look at me. KC was sitting beside her.

By then I was sure the whole thing was a big joke—it was all a little too dramatic, a little overplayed—but I couldn't decide whether on me or for. If the former, well and good, but why and to what end? If the latter, how was I supposed to play along? More importantly, if the joke was *for* me, it had to be *on* KC, so how had they gotten him to play along, because he definitely seemed to be playing along.

"Guys," said KC, "don't be so hard on him. He's okay." He turned to me. "You're okay, right?"

It didn't sound like he was checking in on me; it sounded like he was telling me. I didn't know if I was okay.

"I'm okay," I said.

"See?" said KC. "He's okay. We're okay."

"Okay," said April, "but only because *you're* okay."

That was entirely too much, and the fact that she turned back to me like she disdained but did not hate me while at the same time sliding her foot over mine just as she had on Friday didn't do anything to unmix the signals. Either it was a sign that it was a joke for me or it was another twist in the knot. I decided to be like William of Ockham and go with the simpler of the two, especially because it seemed like that was better for me anyway. The only problem was, my razor was only mental. I couldn't think of an action or phrase that would show I got it and was willing to go along, mostly because I didn't get it, so I kept my mouth closed and let my foot rest beneath April's in hopes that was enough.

"Promise you won't do it again," said April. "At least not tonight."

"I promise," I said.

"I still don't trust him," said Bonnie, "but whatever."

Though I had decided that I was not the butt of this joke, whatever it was (and this weird ritual of repentance was only serving to make me more certain if not more comfortable), every word from Bonnie's mouth made me more tense, more angry. It was almost exactly like back in high school, except in this case everything she said had an extra layer of irony that she showed no awareness of, which is called dramatic irony, which is exactly the worst kind to deal with, except for maybe physical torture irony, if that's been invented yet.

Even KC sensed the tension and tried to cut it by ordering another pitcher. I couldn't imagine what they must have said to him beforehand to make him act this way.

"Bonnie was just telling us about her dissertation," said KC. "It's really interesting."

As heartened as I was by KC's attempt to be the peacemaker, as a philosopher I seriously doubted he even knew what a dissertation was, much less understood what it was about, and I couldn't help trying to throw it back in his face like a reflex reaction. So I asked *him* instead of Bonnie.

"What was it about?" I said.

I got half my malicious wish. His face went slack and awkward, but he still seemed to be of good cheer.

"They're gonna publish it as a book," he said.

The waitress, the same one from before, placed the pitcher on the table, and he used that as an excuse to let that be that.

"Another glass, too," he said, "for Knight Rider, I mean," and he nodded toward me, "him."

I didn't want a beer, didn't want anything that raised the risk that things could end up the way they had last time, but I figured that there wouldn't be much left in the pitcher by the time the waitress got back, and anyway, I was preoccupied with the news that Bonnie Barstow was publishing a book, which meant that she was about to be an official philosopher as a matter of fact.

"A book?" I said.

"Yes," said Bonnie, taking on the tone the public intellectual uses to address the great unwashed. "I'm calling it *The Concept of Irony with Constant Reference to John Ashcroft*. The basic concept is that these whiny bastards have our balls cut off since Abu Ghraib—"

"Political philosophy," I said.

I'm not into political philosophy.

"Not really," she said, a little defensive. "It's just a pretext. All these lame reflections on torture got me thinking about alternatives and I realized that irony might make a good alternative to torture. Or it might just be a different kind."

The waitress placed a frosted glass in front of me and I let it sit there.

"Interesting," I said, when really it just sounded stupid to me, "but isn't everything ironic these days?"

"Every *thing* became ironic the minute we made up a language to talk about it," she said. "All the more reason to refine it for our purposes—there's an unlimited supply."

It still sounded stupid to me. KC started to reach for my glass, and I cut him off.

"I don't want any," I said.

"But you drank on Friday," he said.

"And now it's Sunday," I said.

I was being curt with him, but seriously, what the fuck did Friday have to do with anything?

"We're here to recreate the events of Friday," he said, like checkmate.

If it weren't for trying to get to the bottom of the joke, and the fact that April's foot was still on mine, I would have walked out right then.

"What good is that if you already know what happened?" I said.

Suddenly I felt a hand on my thigh. From the direction of its approach I knew it was Bonnie's. I made a point of not looking her way. My pants tightened quickly, and she must have noticed.

"I know what happened," said KC, "but I don't *remember*."

He went back to pouring, and though I still had no intention of trying to help him remember the events of Friday much less recreate them, I was ready for a drink by then. I accepted and took a deep gulp. Bonnie Barstow's hand pressed down more firmly on my thigh.

"I need to use the ladies' room," she said.

"Me too," said April.

Bonnie turned toward me to indicate that I should let her out. My pants were as ill-fitting as they'd ever been so I pretended that I hadn't understood. I needed to buy myself some time.

"I don't have to go," I said.

The hand on my thigh went from pressing to squeezing at the same time as April's foot went from my foot to my calf and I worried my pants would split.

"But will you let me out?" said Bonnie.

"Oh!" I said. I tried to sound as surprised as I could, but it came out more like pain. "Yeah."

I didn't move. Bonnie stared at me like she didn't know what was wrong with me, then let up on the pressure and removed the hand altogether. Things with me, however, stayed as they'd been. I counted to three in my head, slid as far as I could while staying on the bench, and swiveled ninety degrees, hunching over and hoping that I'd made enough space for Bonnie to get out without my having to get up.

Bonnie rustled her bag and made a big production about getting out, even though I could tell she had enough room. Free of me, she walked with April toward the restroom, what I assumed was the restroom. I watched them until they turned a corner and out of sight. I turned back to my place at the table. KC was still staring in the direction they'd gone off, awaiting their return, as though there was going to be some kind of prize for seeing them first. But he hadn't forgotten I was there.

"Dude," he said, "why're you being so weird?"

That was a good one.

"Who's being weird?" I said.

"You," he said.

"*You're* being weird," I said.

He cracked a grin.

"You wouldn't say that if you knew what I know," he said.

As you've probably noticed by now, the idea of KC being in the know about anything that matters is about the worst one I can think of, and yet asking him to include you in the know is exactly the way to keep yourself out of it. It took everything I had not to ask him what he knew. Fortunately it was obvious that whatever it was was too big for him to keep a secret for long, and it obviously had something to do with Bonnie or April or both, and we expected them back any minute, and he had to say it before they returned. I resigned myself to waiting and reminded myself not to gratify him by helping it along.

"Well since I don't," I said, "I'll keep saying *you're* the one being weird."

He looked pissed for a second but shook it off.

"Let's just say you're real lucky," he said. "Not as lucky as I'm about to be, but lucky."

The part about him being about to be lucky made me nervous. I figured it must have something to do with the thing he was in the know about that I wasn't, so I couldn't ask, but I also figured it was safe enough to ask why I was lucky.

"And why am I so lucky?" I said.

"I was about to get laid on Friday night until you decided to go and turn Rocky on me," he said.

I couldn't imagine who had been planning on laying him Friday night. Maybe the waitress, if she was blind and an idiot.

"The punch was for good reason," I said. "You said so yourself. And who would sleep with you anyway?"

He glared at me a minute. He'd wanted to drag it out and make it a big surprise. Now it was clear he wanted it to be more like a punch in my eye, or a hammer to my skull.

"April Curtis," he said. "Fuckhead."

I laughed, not because I didn't believe it. I didn't. But I also *fully* believed it, and I could see that he did too, and that was why I laughed. The laughter sounded like a series of staccato shrieks and it felt like crying. I stopped it as quickly as I could, but it actually became crying. Then I took some time to think how I should respond in words, and it took so long that KC must have been able to read it on my face, because his expression got more confident with each alternative that passed through my head. It got so bad I had to throw out some filler just to break the silence.

"I thought you didn't remember Friday," I said.

"I don't," he said. "April told me just now."

Obviously April Curtis tells a lot of people a lot of things. She'd told *me* some things I'd started to be suspicious of, but what ultimately mattered was what she'd done, and what she'd done was let me walk her home and also kissed me goodnight, not to mention invited me to peek into her windows from the alleyway. In all that time she'd never given me the impression that she'd had any intention of doing otherwise. I realized that this was part of the joke, and I started to think maybe it was for me after all, and I thought maybe I even had an inkling of how to play along.

I hoped.

I hoped.

"None of this explains why I'm lucky," I said.

"You're lucky," he said, "that I'm not gonna beat your ass tonight."

I was feeling a little more confident and was about to remind him exactly who'd beaten whose ass on Friday, but he didn't give me room, just kept on going, worried that the woman of whom he spoke and also her sister could be back at any moment.

"That's what I would have done if April hadn't met me here early to explain things," he said. "Lucky for you and more lucky for me, her sister came along and she likes me too, if you know what I mean. They said as long as there's no violence tonight, the three of us are going back to April's place together. So you've been spared a beating, at least for tonight, and I'm having my first manger twat. Lucky," he said, pointing at me, and then at himself, "luckier."

He actually said *manger twat*, and you don't have to be French to know what that actually means, and you don't actually have to be French to know that's not what he meant. But I knew what he meant, and the only thing I couldn't understand was where in the fuck he ever got the idea that they'd let him mange their twats. I mean, I was sure they'd suggested as much, there wasn't a doubt in my mind, seeing how they seemed to operate, but whatever could have possessed him to believe them, to take them at their word, was miles beyond me.

I mean, this is KC we're talking about. Kit Carson manging twat with April Curtis and Bonnie Barstow?

Not only was I finally at ease, sure I'd figured out the joke, and that it was definitely *not* on me even if it wasn't necessarily *for* me, but I was also pretty sure I knew how to play along. I had the whole night to try to provoke KC, knowing that he wouldn't dare risk ruining a threesome he couldn't know was actually impossible. I hoped on both accounts.

I decided I'd wait until the women came back, try it out, and see what happened. It was only then I realized the women were taking a really long time coming back.

"I guess you *are* pretty lucky," I said. "Where are they, anyway?"

"The bathroom," he said, like I was some kind of idiot.

"Don't you think they've been in there kind of long?" I said.

He checked his watch as though it had some kind of bathroom timer on it, but it didn't have any timer at all.

"Damn," he said.

"What?" I said.

"You owe me a new watch," he said.

"Why?" I said.

"It broke when I fell," he said.

He meant when I'd knocked him over.

He unhooked the band and shoved it across the table to me. I picked it up and saw that the face was smashed and the clock had stopped at 12:01. That was when I knew for certain the fight had taken place on Saturday, and also that fair was fair, and I did, in fact, owe him a new watch.

"I'll get you one," I said, and then for some reason I wrapped the old one around my wrist and fastened it like a scarlet letter or a mark of Cain I can be proud of.

He nodded his head, not, I guess, wanting to humiliate himself any further by making a bigger deal of it, and also maybe chastened by my willingness to take responsibility for what I'd done. I was not doing a very good job of antagonizing him, but told myself it was because I was waiting for the women to come back. I looked off toward the restrooms. They weren't coming back yet. It had been a really long time, but I didn't feel like bringing it up again already.

KC and I sat there quietly, me trying to think about the ways I could torture him when April and Bonnie came back, but more and more worried about whether or not they were coming back; him thinking about God-knows-what, probably manging twat, because after a few minutes I saw him snap out of it almost physically, and he finally broke the silence.

"God!" he said. "What's taking them so long?"

"I don't know," I said, looking around conspicuously.

"Wish I had my fucking watch," he said.

"I told you I'd get you a new one," I said.

"That'll do us a lot of good right now," he said, as if all we needed was a watch to straighten things out.

It was starting to look like we'd been ditched, watch or no. I think we both knew it, because KC turned toward what he always turned toward at a time like that, which was denial and booze. He ordered another pitcher, and I didn't have the spirit to stop him, maybe because I was still holding out a little hope they'd be back.

"For when they get back," he said.

"Yeah," I nodded.

The beer came and we drank in silence. We drank and drank and drank in silence, and I matched him sip for sip. I made it a point, which meant when, at a certain point on the final pint, I noticed him speeding up, I sped up too, and we would have looked, to anyone looking, like we were racing toward some kind of climax. But no one was looking, and we knew this because we both kept looking around, not trying to hide it from each other, but not acknowledging it either, because to acknowledge it would have meant to acknowledge what we were looking for, to acknowledge what we could no longer deny, that April and Bonnie weren't coming back. So we sipped faster and faster until, at exactly the same time, our glasses were empty. I set mine down on the table and KC brought his down with a whack that would have shattered the one and cracked the other if both weren't actually plastic masquerading as something else.

"No wonder her first husband killed himself," he growled in his pirate voice.

"What?" I said.

"April Curtis's husband," he said, "killed himself."

That she'd been married before cleared up the difference between Barstow and Curtis, but I didn't see what difference it could make to KC, as though April wasn't hot unto death whether she'd ever been married or not, and pretty interesting to boot.

"What difference does it make to you?" I said.

"Left a lot of money behind," he said, as though that proved anything. "She doesn't even need the job."

"Why the fuck are you talking like a pirate?" I said, but I knew why. He was drunk and bitter.

"Heard she drove him to it," he said.

"From who?" I said.

He thought a minute, actually tilted his head back to show he was thinking. I couldn't decide whether he was trying to remember who had told him or choosing a plausible source for a story he'd made up.

"Rita?" he said, hesitantly.

"Rita?" I said.

"Rita," he said.

He sounded convinced, like he'd only needed to hear me say the name, but I wasn't. Convinced I mean. I just didn't have anything else to go on.

"How the hell would Rita know?" I said.

"The bathroom," he said, letting his head fall to his arms on the table.

It reminded me of that ridiculous fantasy, or suspicion, I'd had way back on Monday, and for a second I wondered if KC had had it too, or one like it, or if it was actually true. Then I realized that KC had already moved on to the next subject, and while it would have been nice to imagine April and Bonnie having a similar tryst in the bathroom, if you could get beyond the fact that we were at Chili's and also the fact that they were sisters, it was not even worth the time it took to think the thought, because they were long gone and I knew it.

The waitress was coming toward us. I said, "check," and did the check motion, and she did a one-eighty, just as KC's head snapped up.

"You're right," he said. He jumped up and ran off.

It didn't occur to me at the time, maybe because I was preoccupied with paying the bill, maybe because deep down I wanted him to check, that he'd taken my order as a response to his statement, as advice. I just assumed he was running off to piss or puke. I checked the tab, gave the waitress my card, and waited. The bill wasn't as big as Friday night's, but I figured it would do for payback.

The waitress returned with my card and the receipt, and as I returned the former to my wallet, calculated a tip on the latter, and signed, wincing as my right hand gripped the pen, I started to notice a commotion coming from the direction of the bathroom, as of a stereo slowly increasing in volume. By the time I'd closed the vinyl-bound book and put down the pen, it was a bona fide racket and KC had come into view. There was a burly man in an embroidered shirt on either side of him, each holding him by the crook of an arm, and the left arm flailed, causing the man on his left to whip his own head from side to side like he was dodging some pest, a mosquito or a fly. The other man didn't have to because KC's right arm held his right hand over his right eye.

They dragged him past me, KC too preoccupied to notice, the other two both preoccupied with him and probably unaware that we were there together if they even would have cared. When they made it to the door, one of them shoved it open with his side, and they both heaved him through, like in a movie, a different movie than the one where the hero calls the villain out, or at least a different scene. They must have taken MMA lessons, too.

KC was no longer welcome to Chili's, and while maybe I still was, I decided I would never step foot in that particular franchise or any other for as long as I could hold out. But for now I had to hold it *in*, because I had to pee very badly, and I didn't want to risk going back to the bathroom.

I waited for the goons to get out of the doorway, grabbed my bag, counted to ten, and followed KC out.

He was sitting on the curb at the corner. I walked over and sat down beside him, on his right. He turned toward me, then turned back, and it was dark, but I could see that his eye was red and swollen and that it would be black by the next morning. Monday morning.

"It's your fault," he said.

"I said check as in bring us the check," I said.

"You were acting weird," he said. "That's why they didn't come back."

"I wasn't acting weird," I said. "We just got played."

We had. There was no other way to look at it. KC and I were on the same level. We'd both been kicked to the curb even if only one of us had. I reached up, hesitated, then let my hand fall gently on his shoulder. He looked at me again, turned back, and shrugged my hand off.

"Fag," he said.

"Look at the bright side," I said. "Now you can beat the shit out of me."

For the moment, I meant it. Not that he was suddenly bigger, stronger, more agile or sober than me, not this time at least, but that I'd knocked him out in front of a woman, a woman he truly seemed to believe was interested in him, and he'd only restrained himself from trying to get me back at her insistence. I decided I would let him beat me up, wouldn't even reach for my ChlorAmmo, if it would make him feel better. I decided it would make me feel better. I hoped it wouldn't make me piss myself.

He shrugged.

"It's not worth it," he said.

I wasn't even worth beating up.

"I'm going home," he said.

He stood up and staggered off. I was about to speak up, to get up, to tell him he was too drunk to drive home, but a cab pulled up before I could, and KC got in, leaving me to sit there alone on the curb, wishing I'd had the chance to tell him to take that cab and wishing he hadn't listened, that at least he'd taken the chance of getting maimed.

I SEE NOW MY ANALOGY about the hemlock and the ChlorAmmo wasn't a good one. Hemlock was an ending, while ChlorAmmo was a new beginning. A better analogy would be: Socrates had his hemlock, and I had to piss yet again.

I thought about going back into the restaurant to do it, but I remembered my vow about not stepping back in there and decided not to. I got up and started to walk slowly toward my place, and as I did I thought over the events, not just of the evening, but of the whole week. While I was disappointed—crushed even—at the way things seemed to have turned out, because I was assuming things had turned out, that the affair was over, I was mostly just glad the affair was over.

Which was why it might surprise you that I turned left when I hit Pine. But here's the thing, the piss inside me was waste, the waste of the whole week, and I wanted to be rid of it, but I didn't want it in my apartment, not even in my toilet, and really, it didn't seem fair to the city to leave it on the street, either, so I made for April's place, or rather, the alley her window faced out on. And here is how you will know that that was my sole intent, even if it did not come to pass as planned, that I was not using pissing in her alley as an excuse to stare up into her window: I did not end up pissing in her alley. I never stared into her window, either, because I was not alone, and KC was, or at least he didn't know he wasn't, not at first.

I got to April's place first and crept around the side of the building. The alley was right where she said it would be. I saw it as soon as I turned the corner, but I stopped before I got to the entrance, because I heard a sound that I took for a trashcan falling over and garbage hitting the concrete. I figured it was probably an alleycat, but I worried it might be some kind of final, climactic boobytrap. I reached into my bag and pulled out my ChlorAmmo, just to be safe. When I finally worked up the nerve to peek around the corner, I saw KC.

He had his pants down and his dick in his hand, but he wasn't peeing, and at first it made me mad, so mad I forgot to look away, though I wouldn't really say I was watching. Even if I saw it I was blind with anger.

I pictured myself marching forward as into old-timey battle, arm extended straight, squeezing the dual triggers of my ChlorAmmo passionlessly as KC flailed his arms in my direction, then tried to embrace me, wondering why I wouldn't drop with him, until his internal organs were nothing but a burbling puddle inside his wasted shell.

As my sight returned, I realized he had his back to April's building, that he was staring at nothing but a brick wall and maybe himself, and that what had him going was the awareness, or illusion, of proximity. I rediscovered pity.

When he started to shudder, I told myself to look away, but I didn't. And then his entire body stiffened, and his head turned toward me, and his face was blank, smooth, still but for the shaking his arm was causing, and his eye sockets were both black, and the eyes themselves glimmering but impossible to read. The ChlorAmmo had somehow gotten itself into my hand. I dropped it where I stood.

I couldn't tell if KC had seen me or not. I didn't wait to find out. I took off and ran halfway home at top speed, resisting the pain in my body, the pain in my body and the pressure on my bladder until I couldn't any longer. When I finally stopped, hunched over, heaving, I checked KC's watch. It said it was 12:01.

12:01

I KNOW I KNOW I KNOW and you know I knew it then. KC's watch was broken. But a stopped clock is right twice a day, like Humbert Humbert said. The same is true for watches and besides, as soon as I checked that watch I got a Monday feeling, the one where the dread of the end of the week suddenly becomes the passive acceptance of the beginning of a new one. Most of the time you don't notice the moment it happens because most of the time it happens while you sleep, either that or the very moment you wake up. But sometimes a week has been so dramatic that you're desperate for it to finally get itself over with, and the evil genius that is the world as it exists grants you consciousness of the transition from one thing to another when you do something stupid like check a broken watch. It's usually preparing you for one final surprise. Philosophers beware.

I was in for one more surprise before bed, one that would change everything, everything but the fact that I still had to pee. Having to pee was all I could think of as I reached my block, and I was full of gratitude toward myself, the evil genius, and the world that I'd made it so far, or so close, but as I got closer to my stoop I saw a body silhouetted against the light from the corner beyond. The closer I got, the more the body took shape, first a long pair of legs crossed lady-like down three steps, then a back hunched as though it had been sitting in that position a very long time, pale blond hair, the only thing reflecting the light, and finally a large breast reaching nearly to the lap, posture not sag.

April Curtis—there was no mistaking her for Bonnie—was sitting on my stoop, alone, and by the time I realized it, it was too late to go find an alley to piss in, because she'd turned her head. She'd noticed me, and she didn't look happy.

"What took you so long?" she said.

"We were waiting," I said. "We were waiting for you."

I probably sounded as annoyed as she had. She laughed.

"The whole time?" she said.

"I also had to walk home," I said.

Sure, I'd left something out, but I really didn't think I owed her anything at that point, even the whole truth.

"Well now you're home," she said.

"Now I'm home," I said.

"Are you going to invite me up?" she said.

I had a flash of déjà vu. This same thing had happened before, on that very same stoop, except I'd been the one sitting, enjoying a summer night, and the woman who'd come along was not April but a total stranger, and she was nowhere near as attractive, frumpy, in fact, if not fat, and she was on her way back from the neighborhood video shop where she'd rented the deluxe edition of some recent fantasy blockbuster and, apparently, felt the need to stop and tell someone and that someone turned out to be me. I sent my father back to my room, and the next thing I knew the woman and I were on my couch watching the hobbits on my little television, and then, more suddenly, I was quickly losing my virginity while she shouted out Voldemort or Eragon or something.

But I'd never seen *her* again. I didn't want this to be the kind of thing where I'd never see her, that is, April Curtis, again, and besides, I had to pee so badly I thought I might explode, and while I knew or assumed that April Curtis wouldn't have any problem with that, it made me uncomfortable.

"My place is a mess," I said.

My place was a mess. It hadn't been a mess that last and only time I'd had a woman up. It was almost never a mess, but the past week had been so hectic I hadn't had any time to clean. Okay I'd actually had time on Saturday and Sunday, but I'd spent them making ChlorAmmo and being philosophical instead, and you know that.

"So?" she said. "I like messes."

That was probably, no, obviously true. But *I* didn't.

"I don't," I said.

"You don't what?" she said.

"I don't know," I said, and I finally didn't.

She stood up and walked down the steps, stopping just above the sidewalk so that we were eye to eye. It was like she was looking inside me to see what, if anything, was there, and when she finally found it, or realized there was nothing there to find, she nodded, leaned in, and kissed me on the cheek. The gesture itself was platonic enough, but there was more feeling in that one peck than there had been in the whole forceful, grinding spitswap of two mornings before. I didn't know if we were finally meeting or if we were saying goodbye.

"Night," she said because she didn't know it was already morning, and then she stepped past me and walked off in the direction I'd just come from.

I stood watching after her and realized I was never going to make it up the three flights of stairs to my apartment without pissing myself, so I let it go, and felt the piss trickle warm inside my properly fitting pants, and I hoped April wouldn't look back, and I hoped she would, because the mess in my apartment didn't seem so bad any longer, and my father would probably be docile enough if I offered him my bed.

By the time she reached the corner my flow had stopped, and I could feel the itchy warm wetness across my lap and down already as far as my left knee. April stopped at the corner as though waiting for the light to change, but there is no light on that corner, and a breeze blew up that made my thighs hurt. It was getting cold again. April turned around and rested her palm on the back of her hips. I couldn't get a read on her posture, but it had the effect of thrusting her breasts forward, though they were hard to distinguish from her arms and the night around them. The wind gusted, blowing her pale hair toward me and stinging my legs.

She said something, but I couldn't hear her over the breeze in my ears and the brittle crackle of the remaining leaves on the sycamore above me.

"What?" I said.

I could barely hear myself.

She opened her mouth, and when she spoke, her voice didn't seem to come from down the block. The breeze and the rustling were strong and loud, but I heard her as though she were still whispering in my ear, as though she were all the way inside my head.

"Tomorrow," she said, because she didn't know it was tomorrow already.

That left me with "night" and "tomorrow" and the question of whether one was meant to give me hope, or whether they were meant to cancel each other out, or maybe she was just acknowledging that there were two times, two times among an infinite number of possible times that she might have mentioned. In any case, there was no fighting it just then. The world continued to exist and surprise outside of my house, and it was time to go in, not in any philosophical sense, but because it was late, and it was getting cold, and my pants were soaked in my own waste, which was no longer the waste of the week, but just piss, the natural result of drinking too many beers at Chili's.

I headed up the stairs and saw that April was still watching as though making sure that I got in safely, and I appreciated that and thought to myself that she was a woman who would have no trouble getting home safely. And then I thought how stupid that thought was, because no matter how smart and tricky she was, she was also a human in a world that existed, and the universe and also other humans who existed in it were capable of surprising her, too, and there was only so much I could do about it in the end, and in this case there was nothing. So I looked away from her as I reached into my damp pockets for my keys, and I went into my building without looking back.

I had no problem falling asleep on Monday morning. My thoughts raced like they always do, but instead of trying to fit them into a system, I let them be music and the music was a blues I'd never heard before, a syllogism with contradicting premises that still reached a logical conclusion.

She loves you.

She loves you not.

You are not Mitch the suicidal construction worker or an office manager or Knight Rider. You're not even Mike Long.

It was all true, or it would be soon enough.

12:01 Is the Rest of My Life

I WOKE UP INTENT ON MAKING THE CONCLUSION to the syllogism as self-evident as it was true, regardless of which premise was right, and even the mess that was my apartment couldn't keep me from making metaphors about freshness and renewal as I shaved and showered and dressed in clean clothes and grabbed my bag on the way out the door without so much as a nod to my nodding father.

You can imagine how happy I was when I reached the block our office is on and found that the remains of the remains of Mitch had been rinsed away during the course of the warmish weekend, whether by human or natural or supernatural processes I did not know or care, and the metaphor-making continued as an elevator, the same one April Curtis had peed in, opened to greet me and then spit me out without trauma and in record time on our floor.

As I stepped into the reception area I asked myself was I ready to face Rita and the gang in payable—including April if she'd turned over a new leaf and was actually in payable when she was supposed to be, and not getting coffee or in the ladies room doing whatever she did in there with or without Rita or her sister—and then KC, and I decided yes, I was ready, but I was even more ready never to ever have to face any of them again, never even to see them again, except for April if it wasn't over between us, whatever *it* was.

In other words, I was ready to give up management of the office with no more notice than the time it would take me to get out a few choice words. Because I am not an office manager and wasn't then and never was, even if I was good at it. So good that I was sure the office would fall into chaos without me.

But despite, or maybe because of the fact that it was almost over, I wanted to drag it out, to enjoy every awkward moment as deeply as I could, and that thought made me happy and my happiness made me smile and I walked in beaming, which must have made Rita suspicious because she gave me the evil eye, which made me smile even more.

"Morning Rita," I said.

"What's the matter with you?" she said.

"There's nothing wrong with me," I said, though the words came out funny, kind of strained, because of how hard I was smiling, "I'm just happy."

"You don't look happy," she said, "you look like you're gonna kill somebody."

"Well I'm not," I said, still smiling, "I'm not gonna kill somebody. And I'll tell you one thing I'm definitely not gonna do. I'm definitely not gonna kill me. I'm not Mitch."

"*What* did you say?" she said.

She hadn't understood me because of the position of my lips.

"Mitch," I said. "I ain't no Mitch."

Maybe it still hadn't come out right, but I didn't feel like sticking around. I went on down the hall and as I walked, some of the joy of pushing Rita's buttons faded and I felt my face return to a more natural but still smiling position. I went right past payable because I assumed I'd have plenty of opportunity to fuck with them before I got tired of it and announced my resignation, and because, as I mentioned, there was a chance April Curtis was in there, and if there was one thing she'd taught me in the last few days, it was how to play hard to get. Or easy then hard then easy then hard. Well, two could play that game at any combination and pace, or would have to now, for the sake of my own sanity if that makes any sense.

I MADE IT TO MY END OF THE OFFICE and saw that KC wasn't in. I thought he might be in the bathroom, or that he might even have called in sick after the weekend he'd had. Anyway, I wasn't worried.

As I sat there in the empty space, my smile faded. I started to get a little nervous. The anxiety was full-grown and -blown before I noticed it for what it was. I was anxious because there was no one around.

I switched on my computer to try to distract myself and saw the picture that I'd forgotten to take off my desktop of Mitch splattered on the pavement. I made a mental note to hunt for a suitable replacement as soon as I checked my email.

I checked my email. There was nothing but spam in my inbox, but I read it all anyway.

KC still hadn't come in by the time I finished, so I started searching around online for a new picture to set as my new and final desktop background. Yes, I was leaving for good, but I didn't want whoever took my place to be traumatized the first time she turned on the computer, or worse, to think her predecessor was some kind of monster. For some reason I was imagining my replacement as a she.

The idea for the new wallpaper came to me almost immediately. There's this painting of the death of Socrates. He's on this wooden palate in a stone dungeon, surrounded by his disciples, and he's still full of life. He's got one arm in the air, pointing a finger, clearly using the Socratic method on some of his disciples, who are fully engaged. With the other hand, he's accepting a goblet, presumably full of hemlock, from a young man who's using his own fingers to wipe tears from his eyes. It's a perfect portrait of the old kind of philosophy. Philosophy before me.

My idea was that I'd download a jpeg of it, then photoshop a bottle of ChlorAmmo in place of the goblet. It wasn't meant to promote the use of chemical warfare to win your arguments. Remember, I'd dropped the actual ChlorAmmo in the alley last night. It was a symbolic gesture, demonstrating the importance of doing something, or at least being willing to do something, to make an actual choice rather than just talking and thinking all the time. Clever, right?

The problem was that it took me a long time to find the painting. You see, I thought it had been done by Leonardo, so I kept doing image searches of Leonardo and getting that sketch of the naked guy with four arms and four legs. It turned out that the reason I was thinking of Leonardo was that Raphael had done a painting of philosophers. But that wasn't the *Death of Socrates*; it was the *School of Athens*, which included all kinds of philosophers like Aristotle and Pythagoras and Zoroaster, whom I did not wish to be perceived as endorsing. Finally I just searched for the *Death of Socrates*, which it turned out, was painted by Jacques-Louis David, who I never would have guessed and don't think I'd ever heard of.

I'd found it at least, but by then I was kind of bored with the project and didn't have the concentration to do a good photoshop job. So I just set the actual painting as my desktop background, drew a bottle of ChlorAmmo on scrap paper, cut it out, and taped it to the screen. Part of the new philosophy is its improvisational nature.

It was time to pack up my things so I could walk out of the office as soon as I quit. I headed to the supply closet to get a box for my stuff like on television, but no matter how deep into the closet I went I couldn't find any underutilized boxes. Everything was in its place. I had been too good of an office manager, which is probably why everyone had taken me for granted.

I decided to show them what happens when you take an office manager for granted. I grabbed the nearest box, medium-sized, stacked with reams of copy paper, and, with a little effort, flipped it over. The reams spilled to the ground, several of them splitting open on impact and covering the closet floor with bright, white low-bond paper. I had my empty box. Let the next office manager deal with that mess.

I placed the box on my desk, ready to fill it with my stuff, but I didn't see anything that I could properly call mine. There were things I'd been calling mine for the past five years—my computer, my phone, my stapler—and some of them I'd actually ordered myself as part of my job—my paperclips, my desk calendar, my pencil jar and the pencils therein—but none of them belonged to me. In fact, the only thing in the whole office that I could think to argue was mine was the bag I'd walked in with, and there wasn't anything worth mentioning in that ever since I'd dropped the ChlorAmmo in April's alley the night before.

Then I remembered my whetstone.

I ran back, box in hand, to the supply closet, scanned the shelves, and found it right in the cubby where I'd left it. Finally something to put in my box. I put it in my box.

I had to go to the bathroom, and I didn't feel like bringing the box back to my desk and retracing my steps again, so I took it with me. Rita wasn't at her desk when I walked past. It was like the office was hemorrhaging employees that morning.

As I placed my box on the floor of the bathroom and headed for the urinal, I heard the click of the door locking behind me.

I had just enough time to turn around before April Curtis shoved me into the tiled wall, and no time at all before she was on me, pressed against me and kissing my face with a rhythm I couldn't understand. At first I let myself be kissed, and it was enjoyable and my pants reacted accordingly, but it was also confusing, and soon I was turning my head this way and that to avoid her lips and to gasp for air.

She backed off. At first I thought she'd taken the hint, but then she moved her hands to the hem of her sweater and pulled it over her head, and I finally saw what the whole office had been clamoring about for the last week, but which none but me had seen and also which has led indirectly to this apology.

I refuse to describe what I saw, not out of modesty, but because it's mine, my memory, my experience, my final proof that the world has to be right where we hoped it was.

"Let's do it," said April.

"Here?" I said.

"Here," she said, "now."

"I have to pee," I said.

"Okay," she said.

"And then I have to get back to the office," I said.

At first she looked disappointed, not, I think, because we weren't going to fuck just then, but because it was a surprise. I watched her expression change as she remembered how much she liked surprises. Soon she was smiling and it was like maybe she had finally realized something about me.

"You're good," she said.

"As good as you?" I said.

"I've still got a job," she said, "and my freedom."

It was weird how she'd conflated the two, job and freedom, as though working in that office weren't just a step from slavery. Nevertheless, I still had both, too, for the time being and for what they were worth.

“So do I,” I said.

“Not for long,” she said.

“You’re right,” I said. “But for now I’m gonna use this urinal and then go back to my desk.”

“Another time, then?” she said.

“Not tonight,” I said. “I’ve got something to do.”

“What?” she said. “Read philosophy?”

“More like write it,” I said, because what I planned to do was write *The Apology*. “I’ll call you when I’m done.”

“Maybe I’ll answer,” she said.

She smiled. I smiled. We were both smiling while I kissed her on her soft lips.

“I have to pee,” I said.

I went over to the urinal. It took me longer than usual to get going because I was listening to her. I assumed she was picking her sweater off the floor and putting it on. My flow started as I heard the door open, and when I turned around, done, she was gone, and so was my whetstone.

When I stepped into the hallway, I saw Rita standing in front of my desk.

I was halfway to her when she said: "You're wanted in the conference room."

I was never *wanted* in the conference room, except when an office birthday party needed setting up. I was *tolerated* in the conference room during the parties themselves. It was not my birthday, or anyone else's as far as I knew, and I would have known, because that lot got disgruntled when I forgot.

"Okay," I said. "I just need to get something off my desk before the meeting."

But I didn't need to get something off my desk; I needed to put something on it. My empty box. I left my empty box on my desk and walked to the conference room.

Before I apologize for what happened in there, I want to tell you something: I'm not the first philosopher that had to do a high stakes apology. The first philosopher to do a high stakes apology was the first philosopher, Socrates. Before Socrates, people who called themselves philosophers were just wasting their time talking about stupid things like whether the world was really just one eternal battle between hot and cold and whether it was better to have sex with boys who were good gymnasts or archers or both.

Socrates philosophized using the Socratic method, which is basically to pretend you're a complete idiot until you crush your opponent. The Socratic method worked every single time that I know of but one, in his *Apology*, and that one cost him bad because it cost him his life. That's what that Jacques-Louis David painting, *The Death of Socrates*, is about. I don't want to get into the details because it's not relevant to my apology except in two ways.

One is that the Socratic method didn't end up working the one time it really mattered, in the *Apology*, and that's why I haven't been using it in mine.

The other is that Socrates's *Apology* happened under different circumstances. Back in Socrates' time they had this thing called "democracy," and even though we also have a thing called "democracy" they are not the same thing. You know what our democracy is. Their democracy was a thing where everyone, not, you know, everyone, but the white men or whatever, had to get together and listen to Socrates apologize for himself and then decide if Socrates got to be alive or not. One person, one vote. Obviously we have no corollary to that. That's probably a good thing, because I don't want to have to apologize for my life. Apologizing for my behavior is enough. But here's the part that's not a good thing: we do not work in a democracy where people think things out and make informed decisions, but a corporation in which Ms. Miles enforces her predetermined conclusions because she never wanted me as office manager in the first place.

So, to continue apologizing: most of the space in the conference room was taken up by a long table and a dozen or so chairs. All of the chairs were taken. In front of the people in the chairs were small paper plates and on the plates were one or more donuts or croissants and beside the plates were cups of coffee. In the center of the table were several empty orange and mauve boxes that had once contained the donuts that were now on the various small paper plates and a cubic brown box that had held the coffee now in the cups. The coffee box was probably empty, too, since no one offered me any. Ordinarily, I would have been the one to run down to the corner with petty cash to pick up all those boxes. I wondered who had done it in my place.

KC was sitting at the far end of the table looking rough with his two black eyes, something like Zorro if Zorro was unheroic and an idiot. I guess what I'm saying is KC's black eyes looked kind of like a mask and his mustache might have been a little Zorroesque if it wasn't so thick and attached to a goatee, which I have mentioned is called a Van Dyke. There were three donuts on his plate and one on the way into his mouth.

Ms. Miles was facing the wall of windows with her back to the room, to seem contemplative and authoritative, like an emperor gazing out over his vast domain, appreciating its beauty and also dominating it with his very eyes. At least I think that's what she wanted us to take from it. For my part I thought it was stupid and rude.

Also present was the woman in the powder blue power suit, the one I'd met at the college employment fair and whom I hadn't seen since. She was again wearing a powder blue power suit, though I can't be certain it was the same one. She had no donuts or coffee. Her presence gave me some idea why I was there.

"I suppose you have some idea why you're here," said Ms. Miles.

Admitting I knew why I was there would have been tantamount to admitting guilt, and I didn't feel guilty, and besides, she hadn't made it clear she was addressing me directly, hadn't even turned around yet to face me.

"Mr. Long?" Ms. Miles said like a question.

She turned, and I saw she was holding a bright green folder in her hands. It had to be the copy of April's HR file I'd found on my desk. She had to have found it on my desk, too. Or someone had found it, or pretended to find it, for her.

KC's puppy-dog eyes didn't go well with the bruised flesh around them, or with the smirk on his face as he chewed half a donut at once, powder sprinkling his facial hair.

"Yes?" I said, also like a question.

"Then what do you have to say for yourself?" she said.

"About what?" I said.

"About why you're here," she said.

Like I said, I thought I knew why I was there, but it suddenly struck me that, if I was there for the reason I thought I was there, something was off. They invite the whole office to meetings; holiday, birthday, and retirement parties; and for stupid team-building exercises that require people to solve a problem using markers, a large pad of paper, and an easel, all of which I had traditionally been required to acquire and set up; but not to summary firings for cause.

"I don't know why I'm here," I said.

The woman in the powder blue power suit stood facing Ms. Miles.

"This is entirely inappropriate," she said, "and if it goes any further it may be actionable."

"Not nearly as inappropriate or actionable as what he's done," said Ms. Miles.

I knew what I'd done. You know what I've done. But I wanted to know what she knew.

"What have I done?" I said.

Ms. Miles placed the green folder on the table between herself and KC.

"The floor is open," she said.

The woman in the powder blue power suit sat down hesitantly. Everyone at the table glanced between her and Ms. Miles. None of them would look my way. They were trying to decide between appropriate-unactionableness and getting their revenge on me. KC's eyes finally stopped on Ms. Miles, and he stood.

"Mike Long used the confidential information contained in that folder," he said, pointing to April's HR file, without explaining how he knew there was confidential information inside, "to stalk April Curtis, which led directly to the injuries I've sustained."

He sat back down. Ms. Miles bowed her head as though to briefly mourn KC's condition, and then raised her head and said: "Anyone else?"

Everyone went back to playing ping-pong with their eyes. Everyone but KC, Edward, and me. KC shot Edward a look. Edward received it. I watched it, knowing the fix was in. Edward stood, clearly coerced. He seemed even twitchier than ever now that I had his happy hour posture for contrast. The beer had really loosened him up, if only for an evening.

"Mike Long stole my potato chips early last week," he said, "and also caused me to spill scalding coffee on my lap."

I had stolen one chip. And then he'd offered me the bag.

He sat down quickly, staring at the table, obviously ashamed of himself, finally fully unmanned. But that seemed to have opened the floodgates, because Cindy stood before Ms. Miles could ask for more volunteers.

"When he spilled the coffee on Edward, he laughed at him," said Cindy.

I hadn't spilled the coffee, but I didn't have time to object because Fong was already standing to back Cindy up.

"And then demanded that we buy coffee for him!" he said.

All Karen could bring herself to say was: "And the yelling!"

After that it was a free-for-all. They took turns trashing my character and making me out to be a terrible person. One of them said she sometimes smelled booze on my breath, even first thing in the morning. Another thought I might be on drugs. A guy from accounting said I broke office dress code by not wearing a tie and just who did I think I was? Voices were raised and skin got damp and blotchy until the torrent of abuse slowed to a trickle and Rita rose from her chair, slowly and with great difficulty.

"Mike Long spends an inordinate amount of time hovering outside of the women's restroom," she said. "Even his smile makes me feel unsafe."

She sat back down with a kind of QED finality. Everyone felt better, everyone but me. Ms. Miles looked my way, and they all followed suit.

"Do you have anything to say for yourself, Mr. Long?"

The floor was mine. It was my turn to stand up and deliver my apology in the manner of Socrates without the Socratic method and therefore to win. I thought about all that I could bring up—that the file had just appeared on my desk, that even if you called what I'd done to April stalking, she hadn't minded and she'd admitted to stalking me too, and KC had stalked the both of us whether he admitted it or not, culminating in a climax in the alley behind April's apartment, and one of those black eyes wasn't even my fault, that if you thought about the whole weekend from a philosophical perspective, it was all one big series of surprises designed by no one at all, to remind us that we existed and to delight us.

I was already standing. I stood there. KC seemed to be winking as he took a sip of his coffee. I wondered if April had brought it for him, for everyone, but April wasn't there. When was she ever where she was supposed to be? It was disappointing. Or that other one. Heartbreaking.

"Where's April?" I said.

The smile left Ms. Miles's face, but she answered calmly, at first at least.

"Do you think I'd let you anywhere near her after what we've just heard here?" she said.

That didn't answer my question.

"But did she say I did anything wrong?" I asked. "Or was it just these idiots."

She scowled. She didn't raise her voice, but her tone seethed when she answered.

"What. Bloody. Difference. Does. It. Make," she said.

And then she brought her fist down toward the table, axe-handle style. It would have been a badass businessman move, but she didn't notice KC's donuts. He still had a jelly and a Boston Cream left. Her hand should have landed with a bang, but it barely made a thud, and then the donuts oozed, crimson and custard splurting out toward the middle of the table. KC reached out, probably to salvage the donuts, and spilled his coffee. It splashed all over his lap and dripped off the edge of the table to the carpet with a steady tap tap tap.

"I'm sorry, Kit," said Ms. Miles.

KC looked back and up into her eyes.

"No worries, Ms. Miles," he said. "I've got it all taken care of."

He popped open his briefcase and pulled out a wad of napkins and a bottle of ChlorAmmo. It was my ChlorAmmo—the same customized bottle, the same chemicals—I was sure. I'd left it in the alley the night before, which meant he knew I'd been there. But he also knew what ChlorAmmo was capable of, so what was he doing?

As he pointed the dual nozzles at the mess on the table, I imagined jets of ammonia and bleach hitting the surface, colliding, effervescing. I imagined KC leaning over to observe the curious effect, and therefore being the first to inhale the chlorine gas. I imagined others leaning in, maybe Ms. Miles giving the bottle a squirt herself, before realizing what that gas was already doing to KC, what it was just starting to do to the rest of them, which was to enter their respiratory tracts and bond with the oxygen there, liquefying into hydrochloric acid all the way to their lungs, melting them slowly and painfully from the inside out. I imagined panic setting in at my end of the room as the first grimaces appeared on the faces opposite us, hands clutching chests, but surprisingly no screams because the larynxes and diaphragms and airwaves have been burned to ooze. I imagined shrieks to either side of me as the gas spread. I imagined slipping out of the room unnoticed and closing the door gently behind me. I imagined tearing my jacket off and shoving it as best as I could into the space between the bottom of the door and the floor. I imagined going to the lounge and grabbing a chair without wheels and wedging it under the doorknob. I imagined wiping the sweat from my forehead. I imagined waiting for the screaming and thumping and clanking to die down on the other side, putting my jacket back on, and replacing the chair before walking down the hall. I imagined the elevator opening the moment I pushed the button. I imagined descending to street level and emerging into the city, completely free for the first time ever. But out there on the street in my imagination, I didn't feel free after all. I felt trapped, like the skyscrapers were just the bars of the world's largest prison cell, the prison of the world. And anyway, a couple of squirts probably wouldn't be enough to clean up the whole mess.

So I imagined myself back in reality, all the way back before the first squirt. I imagined trying to get closer, being the first to inhale. The room was too crowded to walk around the table, so I imagined jumping up on the table, running all the way down, lunging like a runner toward second base, grabbing the bottle from KC's paws and raising it above my head, standing, squirting it in the air like a bottle of champagne after a World Series win. I imagined dancing on the table while the fire consumed me, until the whole damn mess was cleaned up.

I imagined it all, and it was good.

It was good that I imagined it, but here's the thing:

I did not want to have my own mess cleaned up just then. And I was happy to notice that I didn't want anyone else's mess cleaned up either. That's the only reason I can think of that I'm glad April wasn't there—if she'd been sitting in the room, even if she was sitting next to KC, even if she'd been sitting next to KC and making a big production of massaging his thigh or tousling his hair or sticking her tongue in his ear, I could have held on to the possibility that it was just another one of her games, and whether it made me want to scream or made me like her more or both, I would not have wanted her mess cleaned up there, then, with them, and I would have stopped it for her sake and for her sake only. But with April missing as usual, there was no one in the room I cared for, no one I didn't hate, maybe even including myself, or the person I'd been, and yet, even with the opportunity to get away with the perfect crime, even at the moment when KC and Ms. Miles were preparing to enjoy my humiliation, I did not want a single internal organ in that room to boil. And that cleared up a lot of messes for me. But there was one mess left—the possibility that that mess might still happen though I did not wish it.

Why would KC even flirt with pulling those triggers when he knew what would happen? Did he have his own mess to clean up? Something more than pulverized pastry?

I couldn't just tell him not to squeeze, first because I knew he wouldn't listen to me, and second because explaining why he shouldn't would make me sound like a madman. So just like in my imagination, I leapt onto the table without saying a word.

I wobbled a little as I landed, but I steadied myself, crouched low to keep my balance, and started down the table. I was still a few feet from KC when the tip of my shoe hit a seam in the table. At least that's what the report said. I think I might have been tripped.

I had too much momentum to stay upright. I turned my fall into one of the rolls that I'd seen KC practice in MMA class and came to a stop with my right cheek flat against mahogany-stained composite, my eyes perpendicular to KC's potbelly, my face smeared with donut guts.

My left hand was trapped beneath my thigh. With my right I reached behind the back of my head for the bottle. As my fingers gripped it, I felt KC's fingers grip my wrist, and then I saw the sausage-like fingers of his other hand forming a fist accented by his high school ring, its green birthstone glinting in the light from the fluorescents. The fingers around my wrist tightened and pulled my arm toward the table, slamming my hand against it until I released the bottle and then just holding it there firmly so that I thought my arm might pop out of the shoulder socket.

The last thing I saw was KC's fist swinging back like a pendulum and then flying toward my face. And that, beginning with my leap to the table and ending with a blackout, was my apology, my real apology. All the rest was just preliminary, unscientific throat-clearing.

Concluding Unscientific Postscript to the Apology

In the "Apology," the original one, Socrates got the chance to propose his own sentence. He'd just been convicted, and the prosecutor, Miletus, wanted the death penalty. Socrates insisted that he should be rewarded for what he'd done, which was, according to the people of Athens, corrupt the youth. He said he deserved "free maintenance at the State's expense." They had this place, the Prytaneum, that was a combination community center and hotel for people who had rendered the city extraordinary services, Olympians and assassins and such. The people of Athens didn't think Socrates belonged in that company and voted to put him to death.

But that's an oversimplification.

If you read Socrates's speech, you can tell he's trying to provoke them. There's a whole bunch of passive aggressive garbage about what a great man he is, and how history and the gods will judge the city that would even consider convicting him. In the first place, it's just not a good look to talk about yourself like that. In the last place, it's clear that he never wanted to get put up in the Prytaneum anyway. You don't get what you want by asking for it directly; you get it by blocking off every other option, and Socrates got what he wanted. He wanted to die.

I, on the other hand, did not and do not want to die, not yet, at least, not soon. I did, however, want to be put up in the Prytaneum. My state does not have a Prytaneum, but there are ways to get free maintenance at the state's expense. The idea came from a little talk I had with April Curtis.

It's just like on TV; they let you have a phone call if you ask for one. I called April because I wanted to hear her voice and because, as you know, my father doesn't answer the phone and my mother blocked my number long before I had anything to apologize for.

April said: "How'd you get this number?"

"Remember?" I said. "Your HR file."

"Are you calling from jail?" she said.

"I'm being charged with misdemeanor stalking, simple assault, and planning a terrorist attack," I said.

"I guess I won't be seeing you for a while," she said.

She didn't sound disappointed, but it was a disappointed kind of thing to say, or at least to hear. I tried to console her and myself.

"It won't be too long," I said. "As soon as I get some paper and a pen I'll be able to write out my apology. That should explain everything."

"If it's good, you could show it to Bonnie," she said. "Maybe she could help you get it published or something. But it would have to be good. You should take your time on it."

She was right. A philosopher shouldn't just toss off his first apology in order to get out of jail. He should, if the circumstances allow, remain in jail, which can provide him the time and leisure to write the very best apology of which he's capable.

Circumstances allowed a little more time than I expected. I would have been happy to plead guilty to the stalking and assault charges, even though they were mostly bullshit, because they would have gotten me a few months' time in county. But the chemical weapon thing, dumb as it was, stuck, and stubbornly. And even the minimum sentence for something like that lasts much longer than it would take to write even the very best apology. But they had me. I *had* invented ChlorAmmo and I *had* told KC about it and I *had* designed an ad campaign for it and left it on my desktop only minutes before I tried to wrestle it from KC's hands.

But why was it in KC's hands in the first place? Entrapment? Had he actually tricked me? I'll never know, because I couldn't let it go to trial. If KC were to have testified that he'd found the bottle in my bag at work rather than in the alley behind April's apartment where he had masturbated, and if my coworkers were to have testified that I'd clearly been deranged, that it looked like I'd jumped on the table intent on grabbing the bottle from KC and melting them all, I could have spent the rest of my life in here. It would have been perjury, but I wouldn't have, and still won't, put it past them. Any of them.

Fortunately, my public defender got me a deal where they'd drop the terrorism charges if I'd plead guilty to felony stalking and aggravated assault. I accepted, was sentenced to three-and-a-half years, and will probably do two.

As I prepare to send these pages to Bonnie Barstow, I've been inside for just over eleven months. I'm already feeling something like nostalgia for the present. I don't want to leave. For one, I've got an idea for another treatise. I'm calling it *On the Art of Love and Seduction*, and I'm worried that I won't have time to finish. I know the public will want a follow-up to this apology.

But there's another, bigger reason I don't want to leave. Yes, it is good for a philosopher to be in the world, and I like being in it, but a nice, cozy cell is perfect for after you've done the philosophy, when all that's left is to actually write it up. You'll think I'm rationalizing, but consider that brief, imaginary moment as KC pointed the ChlorAmmo bottle at the mess he, I, we all had made. Remember how I walked out onto the street after the imaginary massacre by omission, how I felt trapped by the city, imprisoned by the skyscrapers, held hostage in the open air. These bars here, though? They're not holding me in; they're keeping everything else out. I feel free for the first time ever.

In a sense, my father was right after all. This is a retreat. Not in his sense of a strategic withdrawal, but in my sense of a place of refuge and some well-earned privacy. And if I ever need another retreat, I know what it takes, and I have what it takes, to get it. I may be terror's son, but that doesn't mean I have to lose. War without end, right? Amen, amen.

Fin